Not another Zombie Book

D.B. Randelia

Dedication

For my mother and father who made me who I am.

For my wife and children who made me want to be more.

For the friends and family that encouraged me along the way.

None of them are to be blamed for the creation of this silly book.

To the guy who always leaves a review complaining about grammar and punctuation, nobody likes you.

Contents

Chapter 1: The Beginning

I always thought the end of the world would come with a bang, but as I stood on my porch, watching the sun set over the quiet, rural landscape, I realized it was more likely to come with a whisper. My name is Hunter Slade. All right, I wish my name was something cool like Hunter Slade. My name is Jack Emily, and for the past decade, I've been preparing for a disaster that I hoped would never come. It all started after the economic collapse of 2008. I watched friends lose their jobs, their homes, and their sanity. I swore I'd never be caught off guard like that.

I was a decent looking guy for a forty-five-year-old man, somewhat athletic and active. After hitting forty I gained a little weight but was still on the lean side. I had a full head of black hair with a trim beard and mustache.

A lot has changed in the last three years. Ten years ago, I moved to the backwoods of Florida. The plan was to build a life insulated from the turbulent world with my wife, Emily. Yes, that made my wife's name Emily Emily. That was unfortunate. She supported my decision to move out to the country, though she didn't always understand my obsession. We bought a brick ranch house on a secluded hill surrounded by forest. We slowly stockpiled supplies and began learning the skills we might need if society ever crumbled. Now, Emily's gone, she left with a wine and cheese importer from Asiago County three years ago. She left me with ten-year-old twins, Brie and Colby. Emily's leaving should not have surprised me, I should have seen the signs.

Brie and Colby were intelligent and very active. They tended to take after me and were adventurous and inquisitive. They looked more like their mother with their fair skin, light brown hair, and blue eyes. When I was not at work, we were always together.

I have worked as a guard at a medium-security prison for over fifteen years. I knew most of the criminals in the area and got along well enough with those that had been released, though there were a few I would not turn my back on. The job allowed me to purchase ammunition and firearms at a reduced rate, and I used that benefit often.

My workday was over, and I was doing the chores at home. I like to refer to home as "the compound." I was feeding the chickens and goats when Cathy surprised me with a cup of coffee. Cathy Fisher was the 39-year-old, pretty brunette veterinarian who moved into a house about a quarter mile down the road from my five-acre plot. She was extremely fit and had a good sense of humor. We have been together for the last two years, and we share a lot of common interests.

Brie and Colby ran up and informed us, "The electric fence is out by the chicken coop."

"Well, let's go have a look," I told my diligent kids. They help make sure the perimeter is secure, and they take their job very seriously.

I stormed up to the fence and grabbed it. After the initial shock of being shocked, I heard a lot of laughter. Brie and Colby are bad children and should be grounded for life. I had hoped Cathy would agree with me, but she was too busy high-fiving the kids.

"You are all grounded," I screamed in a manly, not embarrassed voice.

"But we're going camping and doing training with the Stevenson's this weekend,"

Brie whined. Our weekends were filled with camping trips, tactical training, and endless discussions about the best bug-out locations if we had to leave the area.

The kids were homeschooled but had lots of friends. Cathy worked part-time at a veterinary clinic in Grantville. She helped homeschool my children, and we worked on becoming self-sufficient. We owned thirty chickens, two goats, and three dogs between us. My property was surrounded on three sides by state forest land and had an old well house that we put a new hand pump in. The house had a basement and a long driveway. The driveway was straight and gave us ample prep time for anyone who wished to drop by unannounced. We put solar panels on the roof of the house and a bank of batteries in the basement. The house could be run off the grid if we sacrificed air conditioning.

After the laughter died down, Cathy said, "We better go check my old property, we haven't been there in a couple of days." Before Cathy moved in with us, she had bought the property adjacent to mine. It had a small one-story house, which we now used for storage or where I spent the night after saying something I later regretted. She had three acres with a large fish-filled pond encompassing one of the acres. Her house was close to the road with state forest land behind it.

We got along relatively well with the few neighbors that shared the rural road we lived on. Most viewed us as eccentric but friendly. We did not disclose the existence of our stockpiled supplies to our neighbors. This was the country so most, if not all, our neighbors had firearms, practiced shooting, and hunted. There was an exception to this, Robert and Tiffany Steiner moved into a home not far from us a year ago and appeared to be relatively liberal and antigun. They were from Coral Gables and appeared very well-to-do. At least they made a clear effort to appear well-to-do.

Our closest friend and fellow amateur prepper, Bruce Jagger, owned an alligator farm in Jefferson County. I was jealous of his tough guy name, but we got along well. Owning an alligator farm may sound ridiculous, but it was more of a hobby for him as he was financially secure. He had ten acres of gated swampland with a visitor center / house in the center. He had retired from the army and did not talk much about his military service.

Cathy, the kids, and I met with Bruce at least once a month, alternating between his compound and our house. Bruce enjoyed the kids and always allowed them to feed the alligators before we got down to the business of discussing ideas or plans about being prepared. We all had a six-month supply of freeze-dried food per person and extra canned food, as well as fully stocked freezers. We also were well-armed and had saved a large cache of ammunition over the years. We all had multiple versions of AR-15's as well as shotguns and various handguns. During our weekly meetings we discussed plagues, EMP attacks, social uprisings, financial collapse, and when we got bored or had a few too many beers, a zombie apocalypse.

Bruce had long discussions with Brie and Colby and would help answer their complex questions like, "How do you stop a zombie?" or "How long do you boil an egg?" I have no idea why the kids asked some of their questions, and even less of an idea why Bruce knew so many cooking answers.

At the last meeting we had, I teased Bruce about the alligator farm and his lack of livestock in case TSHTF, until he pointed out to me that his alligators were effective watchdogs and "you can eat gator." By the way, TSHTF means "the shit hits the fan" and if you did not know that, why are you reading this book? Wait, maybe that is why you are reading this book! Bruce not only had a tough guy name, but he was also damn smart. We had a small trail that ran through the state forest behind our house and ended close to the back of his property.

The first signs were easy to miss. A strange news report about a flu outbreak in a distant city, rumors of violent uprisings spreading on social media. But then, the stories became more frequent, more disturbing. People were lashing out randomly at each other, attacking loved ones. It was like something out of a bad horror movie. I remember the exact moment I knew things were serious. I was watching the evening news, and the anchor, pale and trembling, announced that the National Guard had been deployed to several major cities. Martial law was imminent.

It seemed like most people just didn't want to accept what was happening. "Just another media scare," they said. But I suspected otherwise. I doubled down on our preparations, making sure our food stores were fully stocked and checking and rechecking our inventory of medical supplies, weapons, and ammunition. Bruce was on high alert too, and we agreed to stay in constant contact. We'd prepared for this moment, and now it was here. The question was, would we be ready?

We reached out to our neighbors and gently suggested they prepare for an event worse than COVID. Most smiled and said, "Okay Jack," though they did seem to give more credence to Cathy's urgings. Robert and Tiffany Steiner seemed greatly amused at our suggestions and assured us the government would handle these minor uprisings. Robert was sure that conservatives were just trying to make the president look bad before the election. Old Robert seemed annoyed when I pointed out that the next presidential election was three years away. That comment seemed to end our conversation, and we went on our merry way home.

Chapter 2: First Sight

My first encounter with an infected person happened a few days after our meeting with the Steiners. I was out in the yard, reinforcing my fence, when I noticed a figure at the end of our driveway by the mailbox. Curious, I reached into my jacket pocket and pulled out a mini pair of binoculars. Now why would I have mini binoculars in my pocket? Probably because I am a little bit paranoid, though I like to say, "Always prepared." I also am always carrying at least a handgun, knife, lighter, small flashlight, and gum. The gum is not a survival item, I just like gum. Anyway, I peered into my binoculars, and I could see it was Robert. He appeared a bit overdressed for a summer walk, wearing a dress shirt and tie. He stood by our mailbox off the road but did little else than sway a bit. He was not turned my way and did not seem to want an audience with me. Having no desire to speak with Robert, I went on with my fence work and then went in for dinner.

It was just past midnight when we heard the first scream. It echoed through the still night air, a sound that chilled me to the bone and terrified Cathy and the children. Grabbing my rifle, I ran outside, scanning the darkness for the source. Then I saw them, two figures at the end of my driveway. It was quite dark, but it looked as if the two figures were fighting, I heard a woman screaming. They were outside my fence close to where Robert had been standing earlier in the day.

I told Cathy to get her gun, lock the door, and keep an eye out while I see what the hell was going on. I cautiously ran down the driveway and stopped about twenty-five feet from the edge of my driveway and the fence. "Hey! Stop right there," I shouted, but the figures did not appear to hear me. I turned on my flashlight and saw that it was Robert and Tiffany. It appeared that Robert was hugging Tiffany aggressively. She was screaming and trying to pull away from him. Robert and Tiffany are different but this was bizarre. Then I saw the blood covering Tiffany's and Robert's shirts. They slammed into the fence, and Robert started clawing at Tiffany with unnatural strength. Though I did not want to get involved in a lover's quarrel, I could not stand idly by and allow someone to be attacked. Stealthily, I closed in on the couple and hit Robert in the back of his head with the stock of my rifle. Now the strike from my rifle was nowhere near a death blow, but it damn sure should have fazed him. Robert turned to me and appeared pissed. His face was covered in blood, and Tiffany was still screaming. So, I reared back and cracked old Robert right on the forehead, hard. Tough-guy hard. Robert went down and should have been out for the count. I opened the fence and escorted the screaming Tiffany onto my property.

Tiffany and I were not close, and neither of us would consider the other a friend, but she calmed down when I separated her from Robert. I asked if she was okay, and she started screaming again, pointing behind me. I turned and let loose with a barbaric roar, not a shrill shriek, when I saw Robert up and progressing towards us. The barbaric roar was due to surprise, not fear since I am pretty hard to startle. So, I took a moment and said, "Oh crap!" That's right, I actually stopped and said, "Oh crap!" At the moment I was uttering my words of wisdom, the gum I was chewing caught in my throat, and I coughed it out. That little piece of gum flew out of my mouth and hit Robert on the nose, right between his eyes. This caused Robert to stop and attempt to focus on the sticky substance stuck between his eyes. Robert's brief pause gave me a chance to slam the gate shut and latch it. I'll be damned, gum was a survival tool also.

Tiffany stopped screaming, and Robert began pushing on the gate, but made no attempt to unlatch it. I told Robert to go home and sleep it off. Robert made no move to leave and kept pushing drunkenly on my gate. There was little reason to worry about him getting hit by a car or dying from exposure since this was a quiet dead-end road in Florida past midnight. Sure, there was the occasional bear and gator, but that was his problem. Pausing, I told Robert I was taking Tiffany to have Cathy check her out and he should go home. I should have told him to, "piss off, dirt bag" instead of, "go home" but I did not think of it until I was halfway up our driveway.

Tiffany was calmer and agreeable to talking to Cathy, so we walked up to the house, and all was quiet again. Cathy asked what happened, and Tiffany told us Robert had felt ill after coming home from work and said he was going to take a walk and get some fresh air. She waited hours for him to return before striking out to look for him. She saw Robert standing by our mailbox still in his work clothes. She assumed he was here to complain about our target practice waking them up on the weekends and decided to wake us up in return. She walked up to Robert and put her hand on his arm, and he spun around, grabbed her, and bit her on the shoulder. She stated she started screaming, and soon after, I had arrived. I told Cathy about my heroic actions, and she asked who gave the shrill shriek after the initial commotion stopped. Cathy may have hearing problems, but I never mention it to her.

Now I know what you are thinking, a bite to the arm, Robert was a zombie. A much more logical answer was, Robert was on drugs and lost his mind. Cathy was the voice of reason in our house of four, so I asked her what she thought. Cathy was a sensitive, well-spoken, sensible, and intelligent woman. She responded, "Sounds like Robert is a freaking zombie." Boy, do I love her.

Tiffany responded, "Odd that you would say that since Robert mentioned he had been through a rough day." He had told Tiffany that on the way into his office that morning, the business owner next to his argued with him. He said there was a scuffle and heated words exchanged. He had to rush into his office because his business neighbor was "acting like a zombie."

I asked if Tiffany wanted me to take her to the hospital because human bites were notorious for becoming infected (and she could be a zombie, and I wanted her the hell out of my house). She agreed and stated her father could meet her at the hospital.

Our property was completely gated. We have cameras on every corner of the house, and we have security doors and windows with "tasteful bars" on them. Cathy was a good shot, heavily armed and cautious, so I was not too worried about taking Tiffany on the two-hour round trip to the hospital. Unfortunately, we did not have a camera that reached the end of our driveway. As I loaded a slightly shaky Tiffany into the Jeep, I noticed lights at the end of my driveway.

I drove to the end of my driveway in my Jeep Wrangler and saw one of my few other neighbors' truck stopped on the road by the end of my driveway. I got out of my car and saw no sign of Robert. The owner of the truck, Graven Blaze, left his truck and approached my gate. Damn these fellows with their tough-guy names. Graven stopped outside of my gate and asked if everything was okay. He reported he was sitting on his porch relaxing before bed when he heard distant screaming and then a shrill, piercing screech. Tiffany snickered from the back seat.

She was obviously sick with infection. I informed Graven of what had occurred, minus mentioning my barbaric roar. Graven said that explains what he saw.

Graven had gotten in his truck to see what the cause of the noise was. As he was approaching our driveway, while still some distance away, he thought he saw something, or someone, shuffle off into the forest opposite my driveway. He had pulled over to investigate when we drove up. We agreed Robert would have to fend for himself, and he earned a night lost in the woods. Graven reported he could take Tiffany to the hospital since he was single, and I had a family to watch over. After we switched Tiffany to his truck, I reminded him that she had been bitten. He seemed confused and reminded me that we had just talked about this.

Graven was in his late 50s and from solid, no-nonsense, farm stock, so I had to approach this delicately. I said, "Graven, Tiffany might turn into a zombie. If you have to stop her, everything I have read says sever the head from the body or destroy the brain." See what I did there? I said, "stop her," not, "kill her."

Graven looked at me for a moment and then burst into laughter. He patted me on the shoulder and said, "Good one!"

I smiled and said, "Make sure she is buckled in tight." I asked him if he had been reading about all the recent unrest and if he was carrying protection from those city thugs. He assured me he had his "trusty six-shooter" with him. Hey, I warned him, and I am pretty sure zombies cannot unbuckle a seatbelt. I called Cathy and told her I was returning and not to shoot.

Chapter 3: The Second Day

Early the next day I had decided to go to town and see how things were. News reports became more and more vague about what was happening in the bigger cities. The closest sizeable town to us was Grantville. Grantville had a population of about 10,000 and was pretty spread out. Cathy and the kids agreed to be extra cautious and guard the house. My kids are both trained in how to handle firearms, but do not carry their own guns. They both were taking karate, and for a ten-year-old boy and girl, they could take care of themselves. I promised to return in a few hours and keep my cell phone handy.

The drive to town was uneventful, though traffic seemed lighter than usual. When I arrived at the town limits, things got stranger. There were almost no people walking around on streets that were usually well populated on a nice summer day in Florida. Those that were out seemed hurried and furtive. I pulled up to O'Brian's Hardware Store, because hardware stores are where manly men often congregate.

I entered the store, and I heard a group of men singing John Denver's, "Country roads, take me home, to the place I belong..." I interrupted them in an attempt to save some of their dignity. I thundered, "What the hell is going on?" The group of four grown men seemed a bit embarrassed and said they were blowing off steam from all the stress of the last three days. Being polite, I never spoke of their barbershop quartet again and instead asked them what was the cause of the stress. Rick Plumber responded that many of the townspeople had fallen ill, and some disturbances had broken out in town that resulted in police shootings. Rick was kind of a tough-guy name, but after the singing, he did not have the tough-guy vibe, but he did have a good voice.

I spoke with them for a few minutes more, bought a hammer, and left. I did not need another hammer, but it was on sale. I was heading towards the ACME Feed Store when I crossed paths with Willy Smith, the local town eccentric. We have to say "local eccentric" now because "town nut" was not politically correct. Willy approached me with a goofy smile on his face and seemed very excited. Willy blocked my path and told me he was invincible, and he was going to prove it to me. As I was speaking with Willy, two things happened. First, three police cars zipped by with sirens blaring. Grantville only had three police cars. The second thing that happened was the bank's alarm across the street from me and Willy went off. The police cars passed right by the bank without pausing.

I figured it was about time for me to disengage from Willy, get back home, and call Bruce. Willy had other plans. Willy insisted he was invincible and that I should shoot him so he could prove it. Now I never had a problem with Willy before, but I felt it was time for me to leave. We heard gunshots in the distance, which was not uncommon in the country, but we were not in the country.

Willy told me that he had been walking past the hospital yesterday and a chair flew out of a third-floor window and smashed to the ground in front of him without causing him a scratch. Willy went on to say that later that day, as he was walking home, a car came barreling down the road headed directly toward him. He reported that at the last minute it veered off and smashed into a tree. He stated he was again left untouched.

Now Willy spends most of his days walking the streets of Grantville, so the odds of him running into strange events were higher than most. However, the last event he shared caused me great concern. Willy stated that about 4:00 am this morning he bumped into Graven Blaze walking down Main Street drunk. Willy stated he said "hello" to Graven. Graven reacted violently, grabbing him with both hands and trying to bite his nose off. Willy said he fought for his life kicking and screaming, Willy said it happened right in front of the police station and the police responded immediately. He reported that Graven was killed in a hail of police gunfire, and he was, yet again, left untouched.

Graven and I were not close friends, but we were friends and neighbors. He was not known to drink in excess, and why would he have gotten drunk, I assumed, after dropping Tiffany off at the hospital. Willy could have imagined the entire occurrence, but I sure was worried now.

I told Willy I had to go now, but he insisted I shoot him. The entire town was aware that Willy was nuts, I mean eccentric, but this was a bit much. Most of downtown Grantville was now modernized and had CCTV cameras, and the street we were on was no exception. I told Willy I could not shoot an unarmed man, so he would have to take his knife out. Willy said if it made me feel better, he would pull out his pocketknife and not to worry, my bullets could not harm him. Willy pulled out his knife, and I kicked him right in, well, Willy's willy. He dropped to the ground, and I headed on my way.

Now Florida was covered in military bases, especially air force bases. We Floridians were used to jets and helicopters flying over. We were not used to large formations of helicopters flying over. On the way back to my Jeep, I saw about twenty choppers in the air headed north. Things seemed to be escalating, and I needed to return home after a few more stops in town.

The alarm at the bank was still blaring, and if anything, the distant gunfire seemed to have increased, but it was by no means steady fire. I stopped by Stoner's Gun Store on the way to my Jeep and bought one thousand rounds each of 9mm, shotgun, and AR ammo. Never hurts to be over-prepared.

My last stop before my trip home was The Conner Pawn Shop. Now I am pretty sure someone in the 1950s meant to name that pawn shop the Corner Pawn Shop but made a mistake. No one with the name Conner ever owned that store. Anyway, the name has remained though the owners have changed over the years. I got along well with the current owner, Moe Green, an older man with, rumor had it, distant mafia ties. Now Moe was a prepper of sorts, but I was never sure just what he was prepping for.

Moe greeted me by name as always but seemed distant and anxious. I asked if he had any silver ounce rounds or bars. For you non-preppers, it is always good to have gold and silver to trade in case things go to crap. Paper money would likely be worthless soon after TSHTF, but silver and gold would retain some value. Not as much value as guns, ammo and food. I have thousands of dollars' worth of silver and gold, but a few more would not hurt, and if things were okay, they were still a good investment. I told Moe I would buy one hundred more silver rounds, and as I was about to settle my bill, some new items caught my eye.

In the "New Items Showcase" section sat four Japanese swords referred to as katanas. Moe told me they were part of an estate sale, and they were "legit swords, not that stainless steel crap, these are high-carbon blades." Heck, if there were zombies, swords would be handy. Besides, swords are badass anyway! I loaded my ammo, silver, and four swords into the Jeep.

I got into my Jeep and fired up the engine. About that time the bank siren decreased in volume, and it appeared the power went out in town. It was still early morning, but all the storefront signs and lights went dark. I also saw Willy down the street but heading my way. He was walking funny, but I assumed that was due to me. I put the Jeep in gear and headed home.

Chapter 4: Homeward Bound

The hour-long trip from Grantville to the middle of nowhere (where we live) was dotted with tiny towns along the way. Most of these towns do not even have a stop sign, much less a stoplight. So, it should have been a smooth trip. Even if there was a strange flu flowing across the land and civil unrest breaking out in some larger cities, what were the chances this would hit the middle of small-town Florida? It was not a smooth trip.

As I drove out of town, I passed the Grantville Hospital and saw that one of the windows on the third floor was indeed broken out. I drove the backcountry roads as much as I could when driving. The main reason I did this was that you miss everything by driving the boring highways. The second reason was that the speed limit should never have been raised to over sixty-five miles an hour. Seventy-five miles an hour just ensured grave bodily harm if there were a wreck, and the way people tailgated, there was always a wreck.

Ten miles out of the Grantville city limits, I passed a small neighborhood that had the attention of the three police cars that I saw earlier flying out of town. They were lined up outside of one of the houses, and they appeared to be in the middle of a shootout. I was going the fifty miles an hour speed limit, which is fast enough, damn it. I was driving too fast to be sure of what I saw. It would be inappropriate to turn around and check on a possible police shootout, so I continued on my worried way.

I figured this was a good time to call Cathy and the kids. Cathy reported all was well and they had seen the helicopters fly over also. Cathy was quite upset about the Willy incident (Graven's possible death, not Willy's willy). I assured her I was coming straight home and to keep their eyes open. I then called Bruce and informed him of all that I had seen and heard. He reported that he would have his shortwave radio up in case communications went down. Remember, Bruce was ex-military, so he says things like "communications." Bruce really was a tough guy.

He reminded me to adhere to "Cooper's principles of personal protection." This is another educational moment for you non-prepper types. Jeff Cooper was a marine who went on to become a gun instructor, "created the modern gun technique," and was an all-around badass. He also wrote a few small books. One of those books was called the *Principles of Personal Defense*. In that book, he describes "the basic elements essential to survive a violent encounter." These included Alertness, Decisiveness, Coolness, Ruthlessness, and Surprise among others. I had been working on all of these for years, except coolness, that one came natural to me. This was a book every self-respecting survivalist, prepper, or tough guy should own.

I signed off with Bruce. "Signed off" is tough guy talk for "hung up." I continued on my way, alert and decisive, with a dash of coolness. About halfway home I saw a car pulled off on the side of the road. I would not have thought much of this usually, but it was in the middle of nowhere, and it had already been a strange day. The area was so desolate, I felt obligated to investigate and pulled over.

I was on heightened alert and executing the principles of personal protection. I pulled over about thirty feet in front of the car, an old Cadillac. I was trying to be alert and decisive. I went up to the Caddy in a cool manner. When I reached the car I heard, "Hey, what the hell are you doing?" in what sounded like a thick Italian accent.

I was admittedly surprised and ruthlessly and decidedly ran to my Jeep and coolly said, "Nothing." The stranger, a man in his early 50s and wearing a big grin, apologized for startling me. I assured him that it was no problem, and I was just checking to see if anyone needed help. I went on to say things have been getting strange lately, and one cannot be too careful.

He said he was on his way to Grantville to pay "an old acquaintance a visit." He winced after he said that, as if he regretted mentioning that to me. He continued, saying he pulled over to stretch his legs, his cold, steely eyes fixed on me intently. He was a big fellow, and I do not mean overweight. I told him I had to be getting home to my crippled, bedbound wife and triplet infants, as she was all alone and isolated, and there was no one to care for them but me. His steely eyes instantly softened, or was it a look of confusion? Regardless, we parted ways peacefully, thankful I did not need to put my years of defensive training to use.

I finally made it to my road, the dead-end road I shared with five other families, including

Graven Blaze, God rest his soul, and the Steiners. About a quarter of a mile before reaching my driveway, there was a log across the road. This was too much, it looked and felt like a trap. I stopped as soon as I caught sight of the log and slowly backed up. I turned off the Jeep and hopped out with my Glock 19 in hand at the low ready. "Low ready" means out of the holster and kind of pointed at the ground with the finger off the trigger, but ready!

I stealthily walked along the side of the road, approaching the felled tree, looking at both sides of the forest-enshrouded road for danger. I made it to about halfway between my Jeep and the tree when I heard, "Put the damn gun away Jack and help me move this tree out of the road." I had failed to notice Gilbert Fountain, another neighbor of mine, standing by the fallen tree. I then noticed his Kia parked on the opposite side of the tree a little way down.

Gilbert (not a tough-guy, nor a tough guy name) and his wife, Jane, and 12-year-old boy, Timmy, also lived on our dead-end road. He was a work-at- home web page designer. Friendly enough, and we got along well. Gilbert urged me to quit hanging out with Bruce so much, because it was making me paranoid. I asked him if he found it suspicious that this tree was in the middle of the road, and there were no storms today. He did not hesitate and responded, "No." I got on one side of the log, and Gilbert got on the other, we hefted the mighty tree, well more like a large sapling, and as we tossed it to the side of the road. At that moment Robert jumped out of the woods and grabbed Gilbert around the neck.

To this day, I am still confused as to what happened next. I thought I saw computer geek Gilbert break Robert's hold on his neck, then strike Robert in the nose with his elbow, twist around, and kick Robert dead in the center of his chest, causing him to fly off into the woods. I am pretty sure Gilbert struck a karate pose before returning to computer geek Gilbert. Gilbert said, "Was that Robert Steiner?"

"Yes, yes that was Robert Steiner." I responded, still confused. Gilbert asked if Robert had been drinking. I told Gilbert that I thought Robert was a zombie and had bitten his wife, who was taken to the hospital last night by Graven. I told him that Tiffany must have turned into a zombie on the way to the hospital and had bitten Graven. I finished my short narrative saying that Graven then turned into a zombie and attacked Eccentric Willy in Grantville. Graven was then killed by the police in a hail of gunfire, and I kicked Willy in his willy.

Gilbert looked at me with confusion, or was it pity, and said, "I got to go, beers and cards this weekend." He got into his Kia and left. I probably could have handled that better, but at least I warned him.

I made it to my driveway, called Cathy, opened the gate, drove in, then closed the gate. Cathy and the kids greeted me at the door. We secured the house, and I called Bruce. He suggested I be very careful going to work Monday and remain on high alert.

Chapter 5: So It Begins

I usually played the news in the background as I showered and prepared for work every morning. The news reported that the new flu was still spreading across the nation and the death rate was climbing. They also reported rioting and looting in multiple large cities for reasons unknown. The news stated that the National Guard was being deployed to more cities. A new tidbit was also reported that morning. The newscaster warned of large solar flares coming our way. She stated these flares were large enough to disrupt cell phone signals and other electronic equipment.

One of the things preppers prepared for was EMPs. EMPs were electromagnetic pulses. EMPs can be caused by a nuclear bomb detonated high in the atmosphere or solar flares if they are big enough. If the EMP was powerful enough, it could wipe out the electric grid and most electronics in one fell swoop. This would put a country like the USA into the Stone Age due to our heavy dependence on modern electronics. Most preppers have Faraday boxes made to keep electronic devices safe from these EMPs. My Faraday box contained a laptop with an extensive library downloaded on it. A set of eight high-power, long-range radios for communications, a couple of cell phones, and a shortwave radio.

It was roughly an hour's drive from our house to the prison, which was located about twenty miles outside of Grantville. On the way to work, I stopped at a gas station for fuel and snacks. I entered the station and was greeted by an unnatural screeching sound. Cautiously, I continued further in, entering the cold drink section, and grabbed a Yoo-hoo. I then entered the snack aisle, grabbed some Ho Hos, and continued on. I turned into the next aisle, and before me stood a lady holding the source of the screeching sound. "Holy crap," I thought. Wait, I must have said that out loud because the lady looked at me offended. Still shook up, I thought to myself, "She's holding a zombie baby." Damn it, I must have said that out loud too!

Before me stood a tall, rather homely lady holding the most hideous baby I'd ever seen. It had large, unblinking eyes that were too close together. The baby's skin was a pasty white with a greenish hue. It must have been a girl since she was in a pink blanket. The baby let out another inhuman cry. I dropped my Ho Hos and Yoo-hoo, threw the cashier a twenty, and ran out the door. I got in the Jeep and drove to the prison. I sat in the parking lot trying to calm down. Seeing a baby that grotesque shakes even a strong man. The poor mother probably just could not accept that she was holding a toothless, screeching baby zombie. No way could a baby be that homely and not be afflicted with something bad.

I went to work at the prison as usual, but nothing else that day was "as usual." I entered the prison and placed my belongings in my locker. I reported to B Block and was informed that all the blocks had been placed on lockdown to stop the spread of the flu that had arrived over the weekend. I asked Melvin, the guard I was replacing, if any of the inmates had gotten violent or were biting each other. Melvin gave me a confused look and said, "No, there had been no biting."

"Yet," I responded under my breath. Melvin left the monitor room without further comment, shaking his head as he went.

I viewed the monitors, and though the prisoners were all in their two-person cells, I could detect that some of them were behaving differently. Things were calm for the first hour of my eight-hour shift. Then all hell broke loose. The relatively quiet day was shattered by a deep voice screaming in pain. There was a commotion in one of the two-person cells. I pressed the alert button, which automatically notified the Special Response Team (SRT) to report to my block. The team of four burst into the cell and separated the two dueling inmates. A lot of blood and one missing ear later, it was believed that one of the inmates bit off and ate the ear of the other inmate during the fight. We had to assume it was eaten since there was no sign of it! Of course, the two inmates in question also had the flu. Enough was enough, all the signs were there, this was the early stage of the zombie apocalypse. I knew I had to act fast to get the jump on this.

I have seniority at the prison, or I would probably not have gotten my last-minute request to take two weeks off. I was informed by my supervisor that I could be called back in if staffing was needed due to the flu. When I finished my shift, I packed my locker contents into a gym bag (Ho Hos and Yoo-hoos), and ran to my Jeep. I figured it was only a matter of time before the rioting and zombies hit here and everywhere in force.

I stopped at the same gas station I hit on the way in. When I entered, the guy behind the counter said, "What the hell did you say to my wife this morning, and why did you drop your drink and run, dumbass?" I felt sorry for the guy, he obviously did not know his baby "turned"... and the baby did kind of look like the ugly counter guy. He also had pasty white skin with a greenish hue. Maybe he was infected too.

I apologized and asked if his baby was okay? He seemed confused and said, "Why wouldn't she be okay?" Denial can be tragic. I said I thought she was sick due to the screeching and that she was lovely. This appeased the ugly counter guy, and I loaded up on all the Ho Hos and Yoo-hoos they had. As an afterthought, I also bought a bunch of gum. I filled up my tank and headed for home. I needed to contact Bruce and fortify.

The drive home was eerily quiet. Even though we lived in the middle of nowhere, I would always pass a few cars on the way. The ride home that day, I rarely saw a car. Closer to where we lived, I started seeing signs posted along the road. What the hell was "Hippie Fest 2024?" Must have been some camping event close by. Damn hippies. I was listening to the news on the radio and just reached my driveway when the Jeep died. I tried to restart it, but nothing happened when I turned the key. Maybe those sun flares hit the earth and all electronics were fried, or maybe I should have gotten a new battery like Dale at the auto shop recommended last week. I pushed the Jeep to the front of my gate, took out my go bag, Ho Hos, and Yoo-hoos, and went back for the gum, then trudged up my driveway. I heard strange noises in the woods but could not catch sight of the source of the noise.

Chapter 6: Escalation

I tried to call Cathy, but my cell phone was dead. That was more evidence of an EMP. When I got to the door, I announced loudly I was home and not to shoot me. Cathy met me at the door and reported the power was out and her cell phone was not working either. I told her to stay here with the kids while I took the back trail to Bruce's. We have trail bikes for all of us, and they are kept in good working order and all have small trailers that can be attached to them. I got out my day pack, an AR-15, and a Glock 19 and started trekking to Bruce's. It was a little over a two-mile ride, and since I was traveling light, I could make it in twenty minutes easily. No, I was not wearing spandex shorts and a helmet. I am too macho for that, and it makes my butt look big.

I approached the large, ten-foot-high walls in a pentagonal shape that surrounded Bruce's alligator farm. The compound has a long driveway that flows off the highway. He had a black-topped parking area that could hold twenty cars or more. There was a gated entrance with a metal pathway that led to the visitor center located in the middle of the alligator farm. From the visitor center there were five metal walkways, including the entrance pathway, which spread from the visitor center like spokes on a wagon wheel. The pathways were raised six feet above the swampland and had mesh fencing five feet tall on either side of the pathway. Underneath these walkways were lots and lots of alligators.

The front gate was closed, and since it was about 7:00 pm, that made sense. I stopped at a small gate entrance hidden on the back of the property and blew a loud whistle from my pack three times, waited 30 seconds, and blew two more times. I waited about ten minutes and repeated the whistling. About five minutes later, Bruce opened the gate, AR-15 on shoulder, pistol in hand. "What took you so long?" I asked.

Bruce responded sheepishly that he was in the restroom and tried to hurry. Sorry I asked. He secured the gate and ushered me to the guest center/home.

Bruce was 48 years old, slightly tubby with dark hair, a beard and a mustache. He almost always wore army fatigues. He was usually calm and confident. He did not talk about his combat experience, but I suspected he was Special Forces.

Once inside and with cold beers in hand, he explained to me that all unprotected electronics have been "compromised," that's tough guy talk for "broken." He informed me that he took his generators out of their Faraday chambers and hooked them up and then got out his protected shortwave radio and started listening. Man, I wish I had Faraday chambers. Bruce reported that power outages and electronic equipment failures appeared to be worldwide, and though it was still early, the rule of law was breaking down. He went on to say that there were more reports of the flu spreading, and that violence was now widespread in large and medium-sized cities across not only the US, but the world, except Canada. Boy, those Canadians are polite. Bruce seemed to be holding something back.

I told Bruce to "Spit it out."

"I did not want to overly alarm you, since you have Cathy and the kids to care for, but there has been chatter of zombies," Bruce informed me.

Damn it, power outages, deadly flus, riots, zombies, and freaking hippies in the woods. The world was falling apart. Sure, it started slowly, but it was gaining speed. Bruce said, "You, Cathy, and the kids are welcome to hunker down here until we know what is going on."

I asked Bruce, "Are you really crazy, or are you as good as you say you are?"

"You're gonna have to trust me." Damn, that sounded familiar. Bruce went on to say, "When I was 19, I did a guy in Laos from a thousand yards out. It was a rifle shot in…"

"Wait a second, that's a quote from an 80's movie," I interrupted. "What exactly did you do in the military? And I know you are too young to have been in Vietnam."

Bruce sighed heavily. "I don't like to talk about it. I was stationed in Afghanistan in 2005 when it happened."

"What happened?" I prompted, on the edge of my seat.

"My entire company was taken out because of my actions."

"What?" I exclaimed, "That's over a hundred soldiers. What the hell happened?" I demanded.

"I don't like to think about it," he responded sullenly.

"Bruce, I have to know who I am hitching up with so we can trust each other."

"Fine," he stated. "Due to my poor judgment, 125 men and women were sent to the MTFs."

"What the hell is an MTF?" I asked, confused and more than a bit worried as to what he had done to all those soldiers.

"Military Treatment Facilities," Bruce responded with a downtrodden voice, tearing up slightly.

"Wait a minute, what did you do in the military?" I demanded.

"I was the base chef, and due to poor sanitary conditions, the Norovirus struck," responded Bruce solemnly.

"Norovirus, isn't that diarrhea?" I stated. "And I thought you were Special Forces or something cool like that!"

"Hey, I completed basic training, and I am a really good cook too!" Bruce stated with undue pride.

"Holy shit, you're a chef that put a company out of commission. We're screwed," was my assessment. "And no more stealing quotes from Lethal Weapon, I love that movie." I screamed dejectedly. "Have you ever shot anyone or anything?" I demanded.

"I shot a honey badger on my property just last week, and plenty of large game too, over the years," Bruce reported.

"Damn it, there are no honey badgers in the United States," I informed the not-so-cool, not-so-tough Bruce.

"Wonder what the heck that was then," was Bruce's quick-witted response.

Chapter 7: Movement

I returned home and secured the perimeter. I was pretty sure I heard the Grateful Dead in the distance but wasn't completely positive. Our solar panels and batteries still worked fine. Our electric fence was functioning, but only one camera survived the flare. Almost all unprotected computer chips were destroyed, so older machinery and cars worked, all the newer equipped electronic items and cars were nonfunctioning. I discussed moving to Bruce's compound with Cathy and the kids. I suggested we stay there until we knew what was going on and then make further plans. They thought moving to the compound with Bruce would increase their safety, and with the alligators surrounding us, maybe they were right. I just needed to make sure Bruce washed his hands before cooking.

We set up a rotation for guard duty that night. We felt it was too dangerous for all of us to be asleep. The night was thankfully uneventful, since we all woke up in our beds around the same time wondering who failed at guard duty. Cathy and I told the kids half of their bike trailers would be filled with ammo, guns, or food, and the other halves then could fill as they wished. My trailer was filled with some clothes, guns, ammo, swords, silver and gold, and my go bag. Cathy's trailer had her guns and "none of my damn business" packed lovingly.

We went to the end of the driveway and pushed my Jeep halfway down the driveway, out of sight of the road. I secured the gate and removed my mailbox. We then camouflaged our driveway entrance. I found out later this really pissed off our mailman. I turned the electric fence on high and secured all my doors and windows. We fed the dogs and livestock. We began our bike trek to Bruce's, which was more difficult with the fully loaded trailers.

The trip was eerily quiet. Not having cars and planes around seemed to confuse the animals also, as they seemed quieter than usual. Maybe they were quiet due to new predators on the food chain. This put us on edge, and we were hypervigilant on the trip to the alligator farm.

We made it to the side gate about midday. I blew my whistle three times, waited 30 seconds, and blew two more times. We waited ten minutes before I repeated the pattern. Five minutes later the door opened. "What took so long? Wait, never mind," was my greeting.

Bruce welcomed us in, and we followed him on our bikes to the central building. The first floor of the pentagon-shaped building was halfway surrounded by bulletproof glass. The glass-enclosed section was the visitor center. The second half of the ground floor was walled off with a steel door in the center. Behind the door was a large metal-walled storage area full of prepper supplies.

The second floor contained four bedrooms, a kitchen, a dining room, a living room and two restrooms. The building was spacious and expensive. It was able to be completely run on solar panels and generators. The compound was designed so it could function well off the grid. Both restrooms had a bidet in response to "the great toilet paper shortage of 2020." Bruce told the kids they could pick any bedroom but the master bedroom. Much to the dismay of the children, Cathy and I would not let the children pick "the cool bedroom with the mirrors on the ceiling and the heart-shaped rotating bed." What the hell, Bruce!

Bruce then took us to the third floor, which was accessed by a spiral staircase that ended in a small, open air, watchtower. As we were taking in the view, our peace was interrupted by screaming and yelling coming from the direction of the road. It sounded like a good size group of people (zombies?) was headed our way. Bruce yelled, "Kids, get in your room. Cathy and Jack follow me, we need our rifles and radios." We all shuffled down the stairs to our assigned tasks.

The kids were secure in the bedroom, not the creepy one. Bruce was in the tower, AR-15 in hand, communicating with Cathy and me through the radio. Cathy and I were also armed with AR-15s and were stationed by the front doors of the visitor center. The screaming increased in volume as they approached the front gate. Since Cathy and I were on the first floor, our view of the approaching horde was blocked by the gate, and we relied on Bruce to inform us of what was heading toward us.

"Charlie approaching, Boogies 12 o'clock, half a klick out," Bruce relayed to us. Cathy and I looked at each other.

"Who the heck is Charlie Boogie? Its 3:00 o'clock, and what is a click?" Cathy asked on the verge of panicking.

I got on the radio and yelled, "Speak English, dumbass, and I don't think you are allowed to use Charlie that way!"

Bruce sounded as panicked as Cathy and screamed, "One female civilian inbound with multiple hostiles on her tail. Looks like the hippie group!"

Cathy looked at me for an explanation. "We have to go to the gate and let some flower child lady in before the Yasgur's army gets her." If you don't know who Yasgur was, then you missed a hippie joke.

"Why didn't he freaking say that, damn it?" she demanded as she shouldered her rifle and opened the visitor center door. We headed for the front gate at a fast pace and were there in minutes. We looked through the bean hole and saw a young lady in a flower-patterned sundress and sandals running toward us with a group of about ten men and women clumsily chasing after her some yards back. Oh, a bean hole is a rectangular slot cut into a metal door that you can pass food trays through, or if you are a paranoid prepper, look and shoot through.

"I think we found what's left of Hippie Fest Bruce," I radioed.

"Damn it, no names, we have to come up with cool call signs," replied Bruce.

"We can discuss that later, letting the hippie girl in and securing the gate," I informed Bruce.

Cathy unlocked the front gate, and I ushered in the thirty-something, blue-haired, hippie girl. Cathy shut the gate and secured the locks. The gate was solid sheet metal, as was the entire wall surrounding the alligator farm. There were walkways built close to the tops of the walls with ladders leading up to them. Not appropriate for an alligator farm, but perfect for a prepper haven. Cathy walked the hippie girl back to the compound, keeping a watchful eye on her for odd behavior or bites.

I climbed up to the inner walkway to view the pursuers. I reached the top and looked out over the front gate. The hippie army had reached the gate and was standing around looking confused and acting just as Robert had. Damn zombies, I thought. No need to kill them, as they were not trying to breach the gate, and I had no desire to harm anything unless I had to. I was a tough guy with a heart. I quietly went down the ladder and left the hippie zombies to wander off.

I returned to a tense situation at the visitor center. Bruce and Cathy had their rifles pointed at the blue-haired hippie girl, while she had her hands raised, begging them not to shoot. "What is going on?" I inquired politely.

Cathy screamed, "She has a bandage on her shoulder, she could be bitten."

"What are you talking about? Nothing has bitten me," the blue-haired hippie responded in a shrill, frightened voice.

I asked everyone to lower their weapons and hands. I asked the girl why she had a bandage on her shoulder. She responded, "I was at Hippie Fest, and one of the guys said he could give me a tattoo for free, so I had him tattoo my name on my shoulder."

I grabbed some surgical gloves from the first aid kit in the visitor center and asked if I could inspect the bandaged tattoo. She gave me permission to inspect the bandaged area. I peeled back the bandage, and after a moment of confusion, asked her what her name was.

"My name is Spirit," she responded with pride. I stifled a snort-laugh and motioned for

Cathy and Bruce to view the tattoo. Both giggled, and Spirit asked, "What's wrong?"

"Your tattoo says Spirt, not Spirit, sorry," I gently told her, holding back more laughter.

"Damn it, freaking hippies," Spirit stated sullenly.

Chapter 9: Spirt's Story

Spirit was given the room with the heart-shaped bed and mirror on the ceiling. She didn't even bat an eye at the décor. We gave her time to get cleaned up and come down to join us for dinner. She informed Bruce she did not eat meat. Being the star chef he claimed to be, Bruce accommodated her. After I made sure Bruce had washed his hands before cooking, we sat down to eat and hear Spirit's story.

Spirit told us she had hitchhiked her way to Hippie Fest 2024 and had been looking forward to a "relaxing and mind-blowing experience," She reported the first night was laid back and fun, with "music, drinking, and smoking," She reported last night the party was kicked up a notch when some local from Grantville came by with some "special tabs" for everyone that was willing to pay the price.

At this point I told Brie and Colby to go upstairs and play a video game. The television stations were still off the air, so I was not too concerned about the kids seeing something that would upset them. Though they would have to get used to the harsh new reality of a world ravaged by zombies and a deadly flu. Who knows, the two might be connected.

Brie and Colby both protested and wanted to hear more about the party. "We want to hear about the big hip people's party," begged Brie.

"What the heck are you talking about?" I asked Brie, confused.

"Well, you say Cathy's skinny jeans make her look hippy," came Brie's doom heralding response.

Silence filled the room. I was sleeping with one eye open tonight.

"Upstairs now!" Cathy stated in a tone that scared everyone, her eyes on me the entire time. I was not sleeping tonight. The children went up the stairs without further comment. Thankfully, Spirit resumed her story.

"Everyone was dosing but me, I was in the process of getting a tattoo done by some guy named Sleepy Bob," Spirit informed us. "Bob was a nice guy and started my tattoo right after he dosed."

"That nice guy couldn't spell worth a damn, Spirt," my comment earned me a pout from Spirit, a look from Cathy, and a snort from Bruce. Snorts are what tough guys do when something funny is said in a dramatic situation, like a zombie apocalypse.

"Stupid Bob," Spirit muttered before continuing with her story. "Little by little, all the people who took the drug from Grantville started acting weirder and weirder." Spirit took a dramatic breath and continued. "There were about twenty-five people who took the tabs, and they started to zone out. After a while they all began to walk around, well, like they were zombies. The old-fashioned ones, not the fast ones. We were all listening to the music on an old tape deck player since the radios all went dead. Bob stopped working on my tattoo, so I thought it was done. I went into my tent and put a bandage on, and when I came out, they were all looking at me. I got scared and ran. Running seemed to draw their attention, and they started to chase me. I lost most of them in the woods, but a bunch of them kept coming, and then I found this place. What the hell is this place anyway?"

Spirit informed us she was a hairdresser from a small town in Montana. She reported that after finishing high school, she went from dead-end job to dead-end job. Finally, she'd had enough and saved her money and entered a cosmetology program. She earned her license and hitchhiked her way to Florida to attend Hippie Fest. The trip had been her reward for finishing beauty school.

I asked her if she knew how to work a lasso. Everyone stopped and looked at me confused. I clarified, saying, "You know, since you're from Montana." This clarification did not seem to help, and everyone continued to stare at me.

Cathy broke the silence by saying, "Time for bed, dummy."

Chapter 10: A Long Trip

The next morning, we found Colby and Brie in the kitchen crying. They were worried about their mother, Emily. She had all but abandoned us and rarely visited or called about the kids, but they still loved her. They begged me to go check on her and bring her and her new husband, Richard here. I called Richard Dick for short. He did not go by Dick, I just called him that. Actually, I owed him a debt of gratitude for luring Emily away. Mine and the kids' lives improved drastically after she bailed on us. But he still went by the name Dick in my book.

Emily and Dick lived in Asiago County, which was the next county over. It was a two-day trip by bike if I was careful and traveled by trails, or at night if by road. Spirit agreed to stay on and help with the guarding and care of the compound.

Cathy understood and suggested I go now before things got worse. Bruce and Cathy were not overly fond of Emily or Dick, but they loved the kids enough to agree to have them if they decided to join us. I packed my bike trailer with food, ammunition, and a go bag and left at noon.

Early on, I stayed on the trails in the hopes of avoiding people. We were very familiar with all the trails for miles around as we hiked most of them throughout the years. The trail I chose showed recent heavy use, which indicated that either large groups had come through or there was a lot of steady traffic.

A few hours into my trek, I heard a small group approaching, and I snuck off into the woods. If they were experienced hikers, there was a chance they would notice my trailer tracks into the dense woods. I was very quiet and hid behind a dense thicket. It sounded like two or three people talking. They seemed to be looking for someone, and from the sounds of it, this person was not well thought of unless "the son of a bitch" was a term of endearment.

I waited about thirty minutes after they passed before getting back on the trail. It was getting late, but it was going to be a clear night, close to a full moon, and I knew this part of the path well, so I decided to push on through the night.

Around 1:00 am I was passing close to an old farm. The farmhouse was some ways off, but the barn was quite close to the trail. I heard someone's voice, so I stopped, pulled the bike off the trail, and hid. I continued to hear a voice but could not tell what was being said, and it did not appear to be getting closer. Leaving the bike and trailer well hidden, I silently approached the voice. Years of practice allowed me to move without sound in the woods, even in the dark.

"I can hear you'" Called a male voice. Obviously, a skilled woodsman like me to have heard my silent approach. "Help me, please," The voice pleaded from the barn. I drew my Glock 19 and approached cautiously. Slowly I entered the barn and saw a dark figure with a small penlight in the loft high above me. I scanned the rest of the barn to make sure it was not a trap. We seemed to be the only two people present.

"I am trapped up here. I knocked the ladder down on accident when I climbed up," he reported in a raspy, slightly whiny voice.

"How long have you been stuck up there, and what are you doing up there?" I asked curiously.

"What the hell does that matter?" he impolitely responded.

"Well, I may not want to help you get down if you deserve to be stuck up there."

"I'm sorry, I have been stuck up here all day. I heard voices on the path and climbed up here to hide. I left my bag with water in it on that haystack to the left of you." I shined my light over to the left, and there was a bag lying on top of the hay. I shined the light on my new friend and exposed a young, dark-haired, scraggly fellow in a blue hoodie. He looked hungry and worn out. His sunken eyes did not match his youthful face.

"Have you been bit?" I asked bluntly.

"Uhhhh, by what? Plenty of mosquito bites," he evasively responded.

"Don't play games with me. Have you been bitten by a zombie?"

He looked me straight in the eyes and must have realized I was not going to play games with him. He said, "No, no, I have not been bitten by a zombie, sir."

"Do you have a gun?" I asked.

"Look mister I can wait for someone else to help me. It's okay, really," he responded fearfully.

"Just answer the question."

"No, I carry a knife for protection. I need to get back to my wife. Please help me down. I don't have any money or food to pay you, but my wife needs me," he begged.

I lifted the ladder back in place and stepped far back. He climbed down with a gallon jug in his hand. He set the jug down and put his hands up. His clothes were dirty, and he looked sickly.

I said, "Sure you aren't bit?"

"I promise, look, no blood anywhere," he slowly turned around.

True to his word, he had no blood on him. "What is your name?" I asked.

"My name's Jonny. I live in Dixon City, a few miles away. Please help me get back to my wife," he pleaded.

Dixon was the next town over and in Asiago County. Since it was in the direction I was headed, I allowed him to accompany me. I kept him in front of me and had my gun handy. He grabbed his pack, got his water out and drank heavily. He then put his backpack on and picked up his jug. We exited the barn, and I told him to wait there while I got my bike.

Chapter 11: Making Friends

We had been traveling for about a half hour when we detected movement ahead. Whoever they were, they sure weren't trying to be quiet. I suggested we hide in the woods and let them pass, "They could be unfriendly or zombies."

Jonny was more than happy to agree and ran into the woods without helping me with my bike or trailer. I struggled my way to his hiding spot and found him breathing heavily. I kept my light low and mostly covered and shined it on Jonny and asked if he was okay. I noticed his eyes looked even more sunken in, and most of his teeth were rotten. Poor guy must have had a hard life.

He assured me he was fine and tried to quiet down as the group approached. They carried no lights and did not speak. It sounded like four or more people or zombies stumbling along the path heading in the direction we came from. They seemed to be looking around as they shambled along the path. They were either zombies or inexperienced woodsmen blindly following a path looking for goodness knows what.

Jonny appeared terrified and had his hoodie pulled tight. Who wears a hoodie in the middle of summer? Heck, other than a college kid who wears a dark blue hoodie with no team logo on it? Jonny sure wasn't a college kid. The group soon passed, and Jonny regained his composure.

We traveled through the night and got to Dixon City around 4:00 am. We talked a bit on the journey, Jonny reported he was a "handy man" and worked various jobs in the town. He informed me he and his girlfriend lived in an apartment above her store. Apparently, she owned a small dress alteration shop she inherited from her grandmother. Jonny reported she also was a pet groomer. I could have sworn he said wife earlier, strange.

We quietly made our way through town. The power was off, and anyone with a generator was smart enough not to use it in town and draw attention to themselves. Jonny and his girlfriend seemed to live on the rougher side of town. The buildings and houses looked more and more run down as we progressed.

Jonny was leading, and I coasted about thirty feet behind him. He looked back, and I think smiled at me when from the shadows a figure jumped out and grabbed him. I was going pretty slowly, but there was a slight downward slope to the road, and my trailer was hard to stop on a dime.

The dark figure said, "Got you, you son of a bitch." Right as I plowed into him, smashing him to the side where he fell and hit his head against a brick wall. Jonny was frozen with fear. I got up from my downed bike and checked on the fellow. He was alive, but out cold.

"Someone you know?" I asked.

Jonny paused briefly and said, "No, no, never seen him before. No idea why he was after me."

"How do you know he was after you? Maybe he just thought you were an easy target."

"That's probably it," Jonny said, and he bent down and pulled out the man's wallet. "Mary lives right around the corner." Didn't he mean "we" live right around the corner?

We came to a beat-up, red brick building with a sign hanging over the front. The moonlight made it difficult to read, but it seemed to say, "Alterations and Alligator Grooming." What the hell kind of neighborhood was this?

Jonny knocked on the door, and a dim light appeared in the window. "Lonny, is that you?" Who the hell was Lonny?

"Maria, it's me, open the door." What happened to Mary?

"Did you get the solvent? Who is that with you?" Mary or Maria asked.

"Some dude I talked into escorting me. He is cool," Lonny or Jonny keenly reported.

"Ditch him, we have work to do. Rico has been sending his thugs by all day demanding we deliver," Mary or Maria said. Time for me to leave, I decided.

"You take care Tommy, I got to go," I blurted out.

"Jonny," Jonny or Lonny said.

"Lonny," said the female voice behind the door.

I got on my bike and pedaled as fast as I could toward the edge of town. Now I remembered who wore beat-up blue hoodies in summer, druggies.

Let's see, today I helped a meth head steal solvent from a farm. I delivered the meth head to his meth lab where his meth girlfriend waited. Finally, I knocked out some thug sent by a goon named Rico to collect meth. I figured that was enough for one day.

I made it about one block before seeing two figures stumbling towards me in the middle of the road. They were moving slowly and had their arms out. "Damn zombies," I thought. Wait, I must have said it out loud because the two zombies perked up upon hearing my voice and came quickly towards me. I really need to stop thinking out loud.

Shooting would only attract more attention. I stopped my bike and got a club out of my trailer. Everyone carries a club in an apocalypse, write that down.

The first one came right at me. He was a skinny, strung-out-looking zombie with bad teeth. This neighborhood was probably full of bad-teethed people. I ducked his attempted hug, but stumbled over a crack in the pavement and fell to my side. The skinny zombie tripped over my fallen body and went face-first into the pavement. He hit hard, very hard. He stopped moving for the moment.

I got up to take on zombie number two. He was a bigger zombie. Not tough-guy big, more like, I eat what I want, when I want, big. He was wearing a beat-up blue hoodie. Damn blue hoodies. Not sure how his teeth were, but if I was not careful, I would find out.

The big zombie surprised me by quickly lunging at me as he got close, and I barely ducked his grabbing arms. I snatched the club I had dropped when I fell and hit the big zombie on his arm. This seemed to agitate him. He grabbed the denim jacket I was wearing. The 1980's denim jackets are a timeless classic, not like blue hoodies. My club was between the grasping zombie and me. I pushed forcefully with the club and kicked him hard in the knee. There was a loud "pop" from the knee, and the big zombie fell to the ground. My jacket was yanked out of his grasp as he fell.

The big zombie remained on the ground and tried to crawl towards me. The skinny zombie was also starting to move. All the noise we caused seemed not to have attracted anyone. I felt it was time to leave this town.

Chapter 12: No Rest For The Weary

I got back on my bike and pedaled quickly out of Dixon City. It was approaching dawn, and I was dead tired and a little frustrated about the day's events. I got about a mile out of town and found a patch of forest to camp in.

I secured the bike and trailer and took out my bedroll. I did not make a fire because too much smoke would have given my location away as it got brighter. Drained, I laid down and got out a can of beans and franks and ate them cold. I looked down about halfway through my beans and franks and noticed blood on my shirt. I also noticed an entire fingernail snagged on my jacket.

I hurled the can of food and slowly stripped off my jacket and shirt. I didn't want to get zombie blood on me. No telling how that plague spread. I really loved that jacket, but I had to let it go. The trip to save Emily and Dick was getting costly.

I did not want to leave the jacket and shirt out in the open. Never knew if some unsuspecting traveler would see my fantastic, stylish jacket and put it on, accidentally infecting himself. I decided to bury them. I dug a hole about three feet deep and lovingly placed the jacket and shirt into their resting place.

"Hey mister, what are you doing?" came a small child's voice.

I replied with another barbaric yell and spun to face my adversary. I came face to face with a six- or seven-year-old girl in a blue hoodie. She was missing teeth, but I think that was due to her age. The hoodie also had a teddy bear printed on the front of it.

She laughed and said, "You scream like my sister. Why don't you have a shirt on? What are you doing camping in our woods? Why are there beans and franks everywhere?"

I interrupted before she could continue with her verbal assault. "How long have been there?"

"I followed you from the road. You passed my house just before you left the road. Are you lost? I can get my dad to help you," she babbled seemingly endlessly.

"Why aren't you with your parents? It is dangerous out here alone," I stated gently. I am glad I said that gently.

"I am not alone, I have Campbell with me," and she pointed to the biggest dog I had ever seen. Not, I eat what I want, when I want big. Tough dog big.

"Don't worry, he won't hurt you unless I tell him to," she sweetly informed me.

"I am trying to find a person in town quietly. Can you quietly go home and get your dad so he can give me directions? And take your dog with you?" I requested. "Don't let anyone else know I am here." I was hoping this task would get her moving calmly and cautiously towards her home.

"I can do that," she cheerfully replied and began what should have been a roughly ten-minute walk to her house.

Crap, she was running. I kicked dirt into the hole, unlocked my bike and trailer, and pedaled as fast as I could back to the road. No time for a shirt. I went in the opposite direction of my new friend and her dog and kept going for another hour or so.

It was getting close to noon, and I was beat. I was on a stretch of road that was surrounded by forest. I pulled off into the woods and made camp again. Still hungry, I got a can of chicken and stars and ate in silence. In my rush to leave the last campsite, I left my bedroll. I pulled a blanket out of the trailer and prepared to sleep. As I got comfortable, I heard a distant rumbling.

About five minutes later, I heard a large number of motorcycles rumbling by on the road. They must have been old-school bikes to still be running. I had my rifle out and ready to use, but they continued on without stopping. After they passed, I took some fishing line out and strung strands about a foot off the ground from tree to tree, in a 40-foot perimeter around my campsite. Every ten feet or so I had little bells with clips on them. A small piece of cotton stuffed in each bell kept them from ringing in my bag until I removed them. Now somewhat secure and isolated, I laid down to rest.

I settled down to rest and saw the front bike tire was flat. I got up and unhooked the trailer. I patched the bike tire and pumped it up with my emergency hand pump. I got lazy and figured I would reattach the trailer in the morning.

I woke up to heavy breathing in my face and darkness. Groggy and disoriented, I must have slept through any bell ringing if any had occurred. When I opened my eyes, I was face to face with a larger dog than the last one. I jumped up and realized it was not a dog, it was a black bear. He seemed quite startled himself and froze. I grabbed my backpack and rifle, jumped on my bike, and took off, abandoning my trailer and blanket. Drat, I really loved that blanket.

Maybe I could come back for my trailer on the way back. I had enough supplies and ammo in my backpack to be okay. I looked at my watch and saw that I had slept the entire day. It was 8:30 pm and getting dark. Since I was rested, and my adrenaline was pumping, I should be able to make it to Crystal City, where Emily and Dick live, in an hour or so.

Chapter 13: Reunion Delayed

I got to the outskirts of Crystal City around 9:30 pm. It was dark, and no one was on the streets, though I could see candlelight behind the shades in many of the houses and apartments. I was about five minutes into town when I heard a female voice quietly say, "Psst, hey you, they're coming, come here." This came from a dark alley, and I wasn't about to walk into it.

"Who are you and who's coming?" I inquired.

"You idiot, get off the road now." After she said this, I heard voices coming down the road in our direction. I pulled out my handgun and quickly walked my bike to the alley. I came upon a young girl, probably in her mid-twenties, not wearing a blue hoodie, thank goodness. She had dark, curly hair, was well-kept, and attractive. She also appeared scared. "Follow me," she said and took off without waiting for a response. We went a few blocks and entered a lesser populated area with some abandoned buildings.

She was obviously looking for a place to hide, going from door to door of the buildings that looked uninhabited. She seemed to become more frantic with every failed attempt at safety. I joined her in the search for safety.

"Here," I said, stepping up to a darkened doorway to an old disused business. I opened the door and pushed my bike into the darkness. She followed and closed the door. I used my light briefly and saw the building was free from any other humans. "Don't worry, I am pretty sure these windows are treated, and they won't be able to see in if they pass this way. Who are you, and why are they chasing you?"

"My name is Fran. I don't know who they are. I was heading back to my apartment, and they saw me from a distance and came after me. Seemed like a bunch of drunks, so I ran. You looked harmless, so I called out to you. And why aren't you wearing a shirt?"

"I had to bury my shirt because of zombies, and the bear wouldn't let me put a new one on," I explained.

The answer seemed to worry Fran, and she was about to say something when we heard voices coming our way. The building we were in had a door in the center of two large, tinted windows. With it being pretty dark outside, I doubted they could see inside. I locked the door and looked out the window while Fran hid behind the store counter. "Get down, they will see you."

"I don't think so," I smugly responded to her demand. A group of four men approached the building, I assumed they were looking for Fran. They made it to the front of our building and stopped. They slowly turned to the building we were hiding in. They all looked directly at me. Maybe the windows weren't tinted after all.

"Idiot," I heard Fran whisper from behind the counter.

"Hey, we're looking for a lady," stated a slightly overweight young guy with a goatee. He was wearing a beer shirt one size too small, which added to his classiness. Obviously, the leader and mental giant of the group.

"Aren't we all?" was my cool response. They all looked at me with blank or confused looks on their faces.

"We're coming in," the goatee guy said.

"This is my store, and I am closed," I said in a tough-guy voice.

"This isn't your store, and why aren't you wearing a shirt?" A gap-toothed guy wearing a shirt with a local bar advertised on it asked.

I really needed to get a shirt. I raised my rifle but did not point it at them. "Today, this is my store, and I am closed. Piss off, or we are going to have a problem." I was pretty pleased with myself for that response.

They seemed startled and had a brief discussion. Finally, the gap-toothed guy said, "Come on, Bubba. It ain't worth it. Let's go."

Bubba was the one with the goatee and beer shirt, and he looked very agitated. After a little more discussion, they ambled off back the way they came. Hopefully done with pursuing Fran.

Fran stepped up and said, "Treated windows my butt," with a laugh. "Come on, walk me to my apartment and I will give you a shirt. What are you doing here anyway?"

We started walking, and the neighborhoods improved as we went. Luckily, this was also the direction of Emily and Dick's house and store. She informed me she was looking for food earlier today. It had been getting late, and she decided to take a shortcut back to her apartment. She ran into the beer-swilling goons and ran. Then she ran into me. I asked, "Weren't you worried I could be dangerous?"

"Yeah, right, but you did handle those goons pretty well." Not sure if I was hurt or proud when she said that. She said when the power went out, food and work were hard to come by, but the police had maintained some semblance of order, at least during the day. She reported there were some strange characters wandering the streets, and she usually stayed indoors. She was running low on supplies, so she went looking to see what she could find.

We got to her building about twenty minutes after leaving the abandoned store. I told her who I had come for and she said she knew of the cheese and wine store but was not a regular customer and did not know the owners. She mentioned it had a snobby reputation, and she could get cheese and wine at the local grocery store.

We approached a three-story apartment building with a glowing candle in the lobby. The neighborhood was nice, but at this hour no one was out. We went to the door but could not see in because it was tinted, making it very hard to determine what lay beyond. I put my face to the glass and found myself staring into the smiling face of a large, black, male with a gun.

"It's alright, Charlie," said Fran.

Charlie lowered the gun and opened the door. He stepped back and kept his gun at the low-ready position, obviously not trusting me. "He is okay Charlie. He saved me from a bunch of drunks. He is armed and could have hurt me if he wanted to." Even with the rifle strapped to my back, Charlie seemed to relax at Fran's report.

"I'm glad you're back, we were worried about you. Why doesn't he have a shirt on?" Charlie asked.

"He lost his shirt when we ran from the drunks chasing us," Fran lied. I guess she did not like my earlier explanation.

"You'll have to tell me about it tomorrow," Charlie requested as we began going up the steps.

Fran lived on the second floor, and it seemed like there were a lot of people still living in the building, as voices could be heard and movement detected in the rooms. She used a key, and we entered her apartment. The building was well kept, and even without power, the inhabitants kept it clean.

"All I have is water. Have a seat while I see if I have a shirt big enough for you to wear." As she went off to look for a shirt, I dug through my go bag and pulled out six freeze-dried meal packets and set them on the counter. I could find more later, and maybe the bear left my trailer alone, and I could retrieve my abandoned supplies.

She returned and said, "Two choices, I have a blue hoodie in your size, or I have a light blue T-shirt with kittens on it that would fit you."

Darn, this was a tough choice. I am not fond of blue hoodies, and it was summer, but a light blue kitten shirt sure doesn't shout, "Don't mess with me." Heck with it, I chose the kitty T-shirt.

It was close to midnight, and there was no point in continuing tonight. I asked Fran if I would be allowed to sleep in the lobby tonight. Fran thanked me for the food I had pulled out and insisted I use her couch tonight. We spoke for about another hour, and then she went to her bedroom to sleep. I got comfortable on the couch. I was asleep in minutes.

Chapter 14: The Ex

I got up early the next morning. Boiled some water on my mini stove and made some instant coffee. Even instant coffee smelled good, and the aroma woke Fran up. I gave her the rest of my instant coffee packets and thanked her for giving me a safe place to sleep. I asked her if she was armed or able to protect herself if attacked. She reported she had taken a self-defense class or two and was in good shape. I gave her a boot knife and two canisters of pepper spray and urged her to stop taking shortcuts home.

I told her about the kids and Cathy and why I had traveled here to check on the kids' mom. She thought that was a noble cause, and we exchanged contact information in case things ever got back to normal. She said she would love to meet Cathy and the kids, and she could not thank me enough for helping her last night. I did not tell her about the alligator farm or the prepper stuff. I trusted Fran, but that was information that was not to be shared. If the wrong people found out about our haven, there could be trouble.

She said the Kitty shirt looked ridiculous on me and insisted I take the blue hoodie too. It had been left by an old boyfriend who turned out to be a druggie. Figures that was the case. Fran walked me to the lobby, where a new guard was stationed, and we said our goodbyes. Fran pointed me in the direction of the cheese and wine store, and off I went.

Emily and I did not part on the best of terms. She pretty much abandoned us for a cheese-selling shmuck. However, it was the best thing that could have happened to me and the kids. Cathy was great, and the kids loved her. Emily would call the kids on holidays even though she could have easily visited them. She rarely saw them in person, though she had plenty of opportunity. Emily usually gave the kids a twenty-pound wheel of Parmesan cheese for Christmas and their birthdays. The kids liked cheddar, and she knew it, so I assumed Parmesan was cheaper.

I took a five-minute bike ride on a lightly traveled road with no problems and only a few stares at my new shirt. I made it to the building that housed the "Wine and Cheese if You Please" store, which had a large apartment above it. Dick and Emily owned the entire building and resided above the store. The store was not yet open as I approached the entrance.

I knocked on the door and waited about five minutes. After no answer, I knocked louder and finally heard a Dick's voice, I mean, I heard Dick's voice through the door saying, "We don't open for another hour."

"Open the door, Dick," was my answer. Maybe I should have said, "Dick, open the door, it's Jack." Next time I will try that.

After a long pause, the door opened a crack, and the eye of Emily appeared. "What are you doing here? What the heck are you wearing?" was Emily's touching greeting.

"It is good to see you too, Emily. Oh, the kids are fine, don't worry," I replied. This seemed to really agitate Emily.

"What do you want?" Emily demanded.

"Can I come in?"

"No," responded Emily and Dick from inside the store.

"Fine, the kids sent me to invite you and Dick to the Alligator Farm for your safety," I offered.

"The name is Richard," came the voice behind Emily.

"We are safe here and aren't going anywhere. You look ridiculous in that shirt," Emily stated.

"Final offer, come now or you are on your own."

"We don't need your help, and we are staying here, but I have something for the kids. Wait," Emily said.

She shut the door but returned a moment later with two large sacks. "One wheel of Parmesan and one wheel of cheddar for the kids." Darn those wheels would be heavy on the trip home. The wheels of cheese weighed twenty pounds each. She handed me the two sacks, and in a moment of weakness, Emily said, "Thanks for coming, and tell the kids I love them. I know you will keep them safe."

I told her to take care of herself and Dick. She and I trained in survival skills for years before she left us, and I knew she was armed and not a bad shot. The heck if I knew or cared what

Dick could do. I started on my way back to the Alligator Farm, but I had one stop to make first.

I returned to Fran's apartment and knocked on the front door. It was midday by now, and Charlie was at the door again. I asked if he could get Fran for me. He refused to leave his post but allowed me to enter and go to her apartment.

I knocked on Fran's door. She asked who was there and opened the door when I responded. "Is everything okay?" I noticed she had a canister of pepper spray in her hand.

"Everything is fine Fran. I am heading home alone, but I wanted to drop this off." I handed her a 20-pound wheel of cheddar cheese. The kids were used to getting Parmesan anyway, why break tradition now?

"Oh my, I can't accept this, it is too much!" she exclaimed.

"I have another, and darned if I am lugging two of these home."

She thanked me again, and I said my goodbye and headed home. It had been an event-filled trip, and I was glad to be heading back. If I was lucky, I would grab my abandoned trailer and get a better shirt.

Chapter 15: Old Friends

I wanted to avoid the neighborhood where Fran ran into the drunk group of thugs, but it was the shortest route out of town. There were people out, but everyone seemed to be avoiding talking and making eye contact. As I approached the neighborhood where Fran had the problem, the pedestrians thinned out to almost none.

I passed the store where Fran and I hid last night, and the door was open. Not sure if we left it open when we exited, but it did not matter now anyway. I was on high alert in this area but got through without incident.

I was on the outskirts of town and was heading up a steep hill when I heard, "Hey you, stop!" Now I don't know about you, but during an apocalypse, when I hear someone say, "Hey you, stop!" I speed up.

I made it to the top of the steep hill just outside of town and turned to see if anyone was pursuing me. I found Bubba and the gapped-toothed fellow trudging up the street, and Bubba appeared to have a shotgun in hand. I needed to get these fools to stop following me, or I would have no rest. I did not want them tracking me back to the alligator farm either. I got off my bike and told them to stop as I raised my rifle, not yet pointing it at them.

They stopped about sixty feet down the hill from me. I asked them what they wanted. This seemed to stump the dynamic duo, as they had no response and just stared at me confused. Finally, Bubba said, "You have to pay a toll to pass through our neighborhood. You were there last night and today. So, you owe double."

"Double what?" I asked.

This again stumped them as they did not have an answer and just looked at each other in search of a response. Bubba then perked up and smiled, almost innocently. He seemed very proud of the idea he was about to share with me and gapped-tooth.

"Got any beer?" Bubba asked pleadingly.

"No, I don't have any freaking beer. Where the hell would I have beer? I am riding a freaking bike," I responded.

After another long silence, the two began talking amongst themselves for a few minutes. I sat down slightly entertained. They seemed to be wrapping up their discussion and were both nodding their heads in agreement.

"What do you have in the sack?" Bubba asked shrewdly.

Now I was sure I did not need to give these two out-of-shape dimwits anything, but I was amused. So, I continued the discussion. I was curious to see how sinister these characters were.

"Why were you guys chasing the girl yesterday?" I asked.

Bubba responded so quickly I felt somewhat comfortable he was telling the truth. "I wanted to ask her out on a date, but she kept going, and I never caught up with her."

"What the heck are you thinking, chasing after a girl in the middle of a power outage while a deadly flu is going around and zombies are attacking people? You think she was just going to stop and say hello to four drunk guys?" I demanded. "You scared the heck out of her," I added.

"That's how I met my ex-wife and what zombies?" Bubba informed me.

This conversation hurt my head. Any longer and I would have suffered brain damage. I had to end this and be on my way.

"Look, don't go chasing after anyone anymore, I could have shot you both," I warned them.

"Why would you shoot us?" Bubba asked.

"You have a darn shotgun!"

"We were going hunting for food. I never pointed it at you. And why are you wearing a kitty shirt?" Bubba asked.

"Look, Bubba, I am going to give you what is in the sack. Just don't go chasing after people anymore."

"How do you know my name? Who are you?" Bubba asked suspiciously.

I could take no more of these two nitwits. "Bubba, I am going to give you what is in the sack. Stay where you are, and I will roll it down the hill." With that I got the sack out, tied it so that it snugly wrapped the wheel of cheese, and rolled it down the hill.

So apparently a tightly wrapped wheel of Parmesan cheese will gain speed rapidly when rolling down a steep hill. I also learned that if the spinning wheel of cheese hits a bump, it begins to bounce. The bouncing speeding wheel of cheese slammed right into Bubba's head. Bubba dropped to the ground and stopped moving. Gapped-tooth just stood there shocked.

"Damn it," I swore and headed to Bubba and gapped-tooth. When I reached them, I asked gapped-tooth what his name was.

"Cleo, why did you kill Bubba?" Cleo asked.

"I didn't kill him; well, I don't think I killed him," I answered, walking up to Bubba.

He was out cold but breathing well. I kneeled beside him and splashed a little of my dwindling water supply on him. After a moment he started to regain consciousness. Suddenly he grabbed me with both hands and kissed me on the lips.

"Helen, I've missed you," was Bubba's dazed statement.

Cleo started laughing uncontrollably, stating that Helen was Bubba's ex-wife. I had had enough. I planned on never coming to this town again. I walked back up the hill and got on my bike with Cleo's continuous laughter in the background. I continued up the hill, hopefully never to return. The farther I got from the pair, the louder Cleo's laughter became.

Chapter 16: Bear Necessities

It was getting close to sundown as I approached the spot where I had abandoned my trailer to the bear. I hid my bike and backpack on the side of the road and slowly crept up to my former campsite. I came to the edge of the site and beheld the damage.

The bear had decided to search my trailer, and since he did not have opposable thumbs, he ripped it and all its contents to shreds, including my spare tough guy shirts. All the food cans were damaged, and there were bullets everywhere. Stupid bear. Darned if I was camping here. The bear seemed to take extra effort to destroy my bedroll. I salvaged as much of the strewn ammo as I could and left.

I biked for about another couple of hours before I was stopped in the middle of the road by a huge man with a rifle pointed at me. I stopped and put my hands up. It was dark, but with the moon out I could see he had a large dog with him.

"Campbell?" I said.

This seemed to confuse the man, and he lowered his gun. "Do I know you?" he asked.

I responded, "Nope." I quickly drew my Glock 19 from my waistband. I did not shoot, and the man froze. Campbell began to growl.

"Daddy, it's the guy with no shirt," a young voice excitedly exclaimed. "Where did you go? We need your help. My mommy is sick. I like your shirt."

"Who are you people, and drop that rifle, please," was my gentle response, which seemed to appease Campbell as he did not attack me.

The big man laid his rifle down as his daughter came to him. "My name is Maverick, and this is my daughter, Vivian." Damn these guys and their cool names. I bet he changed his name later in life.

"I'm sorry I ambushed you, we need help. My oldest daughter is a nurse, but she was out of town when the power died. My wife is sick, and I need to get to town for medication. My car isn't working, and I got desperate. My wife cut her finger on a can, and it has become infected. It has gotten so bad she now has a high fever, and she is shaking constantly. I can't lose my wife to an infected cut," Maverick said firmly.

Most preppers have a good supply of antibiotics for cases like this. Preppers used to order fish antibiotics through the mail. You did not need a prescription, and it was cheap. Unfortunately, the government decided that was not okay anymore, and now even for fish antibiotics, you needed a doctor (veterinarian) prescription. You could still order antibiotics from Mexico on the internet, which was a bad idea. You could fake an illness and get a prescription from your doctor and store it. The final option was there were a few companies that would give you a package of various antibiotics prescribed by their doctors at very high rates.

"I can help you if you'll trust me," I offered.

"Oh thank you," was Vivian's response

"Mister, a guy traveling at night, during a long blackout, wearing a light blue kitty shirt has got to be crazy or a badass." It had taken this long for someone to finally recognize I was a tough guy.

"I just don't know if you are dangerous crazy. Or harmless crazy." Wait, what did he say?

"Come on up to the house." Maverick picked up his rifle and led the way with Campbell, Vivian, and me trailing. I was asking for a shirt in payment for sure.

We walked up a long, winding driveway that led to a small, tidy brick house. I was surprised to hear the drone of a generator and asked how that was possible. Maverik informed me that he had an old generator that had been handed down from his father. When the power went out, he tinkered with it until he got it running. He led us into the house and introduced me to his young wife, Rose, who was wrapped in a blanket, shivering on a couch in their living room.

After the introductions were made, I asked to see her finger. It was red and swollen, but did not smell bad. I don't know much about wounds, I leave that up to Cathy, but I know that if there is a bad smell, you're in a lot of trouble. I informed Maverick and Rose that I had some amoxicillin in my bag and would give them enough for a full round of treatment.

Both were shocked that I had medication, and all three were overjoyed with this news. They insisted I stay the night and have dinner with them. Maverick asked, "Are you okay with eating bear meat? Since the power went out, I have been hunting to feed the family, and I bagged a bear that had been roaming the area last night." This brought a smile to my face as I gladly accepted the offer.

The next morning, I was fed leftover bear stew and a cup of coffee. We discussed what had been going on since the power went out. Maverick said he went to Crystal City the day after the power went down to get supplies. He reported that he tried to buy ammunition for his gun and rifle, but the stores were only taking cash or trades, and they had raised the prices so high he could only get a box of fifty rounds of full metal jacket 9mm shells and no AR shells.

Most preppers insist that you have at least 1000 rounds of ammunition in every caliber of gun you own. Full metal jacket ammo is good for target practice and will work in a pinch for self-defense, but hollow point ammunition has much better stopping power and is made for self-defense. The only people that used full metal jacket ammo against humans were gangbangers who did not know better. The wise preppers also recommend you have at least five magazines for every gun you own.

As luck would have it, Maverick needed the exact rounds I carried. This was not a great coincidence, as 9mm and 5.56 NATO are among the most common rounds in use. I did not want the nice family to be in danger, so I gave them all of the rounds I salvaged from my destroyed trailer.

After many hugs and thanks, I told them I needed to get back to my kids and Cathy. I gave them my home address, and we agreed to get together if and when this all blew over. I hugged Vivian goodbye and biked off down the road. About an hour later, I pulled off to the side of the road to have a drink of water. I tipped up my bottle, and some spilled some water onto my light blue kitty shirt. Man, I hate this shirt, I had forgotten to ask Maverick for a better shirt.

Chapter 17: Home Again

I biked the rest of the day. Riding around Dixon City took just a little longer than biking through it. I had no desire to run into Jonny, Lonny, Mary, or Maria again. As evening approached, I was passing the barn where I accidentally helped Jonny, or was it Lonny, steal a gallon of solvent. I heard voices in the barn as I got closer. I pulled off into the woods and called out, "Hello in the barn."

"Hello out there, state your business," was the deep-voiced response.

"Just passing through, on my way back from Crystal City," I answered.

"We are coming out, keep your gun down, and we will keep ours down too," the deep voice stated.

Out walked an older bearded man with a farmer's hat on, accompanied by a younger, clean-shaven fellow in overalls. Both were carrying shotguns, but they were pointed down as promised. We took a moment to size each other up. The younger man cracked a smile and said, "What's with the shirt?"

I could not help but snort at his question, and that seemed to put everyone more at ease. "That's a long story, but I will give you the short version." I then went on to tell them I went to check on my kids' mother in Crystal City. I mentioned Fran, Bubba, and Cleo, but I left out the Jonny or Lonny's part of the story.

The two men introduced themselves as father and son. They were the McCormick family, the owners of the farm, and were investigating a recent break-in of their barn. They believed some drug dealers had broken in and stolen some chemicals to make drugs. I am glad I was not wearing the blue hoodie that was in the bottom of my backpack.

We discussed some of the strange people we all had recently seen out and about. None of us said "zombies," but it was clear that was what we were describing, and they were fortifying their property and moving everything closer to the house. They stated they were self-sufficient and were going to "hunker down" until things calmed down. They asked if I needed anything. I assured them I was fine and not too far from home. They were polite enough not to ask where my home was. As we spoke, we noticed a plume of smoke coming from the forest, west of where

I was heading. From the amount of smoke, it was likely a large campfire. Anyone brave enough to have a campfire that visible wasn't afraid of being seen.

We said our goodbyes and exchanged radio contact information. I got back on my bike and made the final push for home. The next couple of hours were pretty uneventful, and I made it to the alligator farm before sundown. I approached the front gate and stopped about twenty feet in front of it.

I was greeted by Cathy's voice saying, "What the hell are you wearing?"

"It's a long story, and I got stuck wearing this or nothing," I huffed.

"Why didn't you wear it inside out?" Cathy inquired.

I hadn't thought of that. "Damn it, I'm tired, open the gate and let me in."

"You didn't think of that, did you?" Cathy started snorting and laughing. She let me in, and I went straight to our room after passing by Bruce, Spirit, and the kids. I changed my shirt and went to bed.

Chapter 18: Catching Up

Spirit apparently fit right in while I was away. She took a turn on guard duty but wasn't given a gun yet. They had continued to give her grief about her unfortunate tattoo, which she took relatively well.

They had seen the large campfire smoke yesterday and were as concerned as I was. We discussed increasing security and being armed at all times. We agreed all the adults would have at least a pistol on them while inside the visitor center and a rifle when outside.

We were interrupted by loud banging sounds coming from the front gate. Bruce asked, "Spirt, do you know how to handle a gun?"

Spirit answered, "I have had a little training, and don't call me Spirt." If you don't know this about most men, if you tell them not to do something that is irritating, this only increases the likelihood of the behavior being repeated.

"We need call signs," demanded Bruce.

"You're a dumbass, but let's call you Riggs," I said to Bruce. He liked that and asked me what call sign I wanted. This was my chance to pick a tough guy name, but I did not want to go over the top. I panicked a bit and went with "Wheeler." Hey, it could have been worse! Spirit was given the call sign "Spirt" over much protest, and Cathy went with "Huckleberry". I have no idea why she chose "Huckleberry".

"Okay, get to the front gate and see what the ruckus is, and I'll go to the tower with Spirt," Bruce ordered.

"Spirit!" Spirit retorted.

Cathy and I again went cautiously to the front gate, rifles in hand. I climbed the catwalk and peered over the gate. I saw an older bearded guy, or maybe a zombie, I was not sure yet, in a yellow and red poncho. He stood with one hand raised and struck the gate hard with his hand in a slow rhythm. I radioed in, "Wheeler to Riggs, there is a lone zombie at the gate, striking it occasionally."

"Did you call yourself Weiner?" Bruce responded, sounding bewildered.

Spirit chimed in, "Stupid Weiner."

Cathy quickly responded, "Leave my Weiner alone." This was followed by utter silence. My first chance at a cool name, and it went to crap. I sighed and leaned back on the top rail, which was shorter than expected. I toppled over the front of the gate and landed with a very loud "bang."

"Holy crap, Wiener fell over the wall!" exclaimed Bruce.

Now for you non-gun people, there are four rules to follow when handling a gun. Treat every gun as if it is always loaded. Never point the gun at anything you are not willing to destroy. Keep your finger off the trigger until ready to fire. Always be sure of your target and what's beyond it. Breaking any of these rules can get someone killed, or at a gun range could get you shunned or removed.

When I hit the ground, the loud "bang" was my rifle going off. I was sure my finger was nowhere near the trigger, well, pretty sure anyway. After I got my wind back, I looked for Poncho Zombie. He was lying motionless on the ground about 20 feet from me. I also noticed he was not wearing any pants. Freaking hippie zombies.

Now I know zombies can't speak or reason, but I just had to get his attention somehow. "Hey, pantless zombie guy, wake up." I am pretty witty under pressure. I hobbled up to Pantless Poncho Zombie Guy and saw that he had a bullet hole between his eyes. "Oops," I said, shocked. My accidental discharge ended Pantless Poncho Zombie Guy.

The others were at the gate and opened it to dead Pantless Poncho Zombie and me. Cathy said, "Oops." Great minds think alike.

Spirit exclaimed, "Hey, that's the dude from town who sold everyone the drugs. He was kind of a jerk and a pervert."

"What do you mean?" I asked, feeling a little better if I had rid the world of a pantless zombie drug-dealing pervert!

"He sold the tabs to the guys but wanted to trade "favors" with the girls. I wasn't interested," Spirit informed us. This seemed to raise Spirit's stature in our eyes. Maybe she wasn't just a hippie. I also felt a bit better about accidentally shooting Pantless Poncho Zombie Guy.

"Well, what do we do with him?" I asked nervously.

"Gators' gotta eat too, you know," responded Bruce.

"Sounds like a plan," stated Cathy.

"I am good with that," was Spirit's response.

The ladies went back to check on the kids and man the tower. Bruce and I took the pantless zombie drug-dealing pervert to the special alligator enclosure.

Chapter 19: Wally Gator

Bruce's alligator farm had one claim to fame. He housed arguably the largest alligator in captivity in the United States. The monster of an alligator was eighteen-plus feet of muscle and teeth. Bruce lovingly called the alligator Wally, after his older brother. He was kept in a special enclosure within the alligator farm. We made sure the kids did not see us take Pantless Poncho Zombie Guy to the enclosure. We took off his poncho and tossed him into Wally's den and left before the feeding began. One less perverted drug dealer zombie in the world.

Wally was brought to the alligator farm after he was saved from the sewers of New York City. It was supposed that someone bought him as a pet, and when he got too big, they dumped him in the sewers.

Legend had it that he was exposed to all kinds of chemicals while in the sewers. No one knows how he survived the winters there. Maybe the sewers did not get cold enough to freeze. Possibly Wally could have found a warm spot in the sewers that kept him alive through the winters.

For a few years, before he was caught, there were sightings of him. Usually from less than trustworthy sources like drug dealers or drunks. The people on the fringe of society that lurked in dark places. Rumor had it that many a family's cats and dogs met their end at the entrances of the sewers. It was said that Wally's eyes glowed yellow at night, due to all the toxic swill he had ingested in the sewers.

No one paid much attention to the rumors until people started disappearing. At first it was just stories passed around by the less reputable members of the community. As the rumor grew, the less reputable newspapers that loved sensational tales ran the stories.

Finally, a picture of the large beast made its way to the mainstream papers, and the hunt was on. There were two trains of thought on how to deal with the now legendary monster of the sewers. Some said it needed to be hunted down and destroyed. Others said he had done the city a service by reducing the population of dregs on society and needed to be captured and put in a zoo.

The city of New York reportedly offered a $10,000.00 reward for the live capture of the alligator. Hunters and animal activists from all over the United States flocked to the Big Apple. Many attempted to capture the alligator, but to no avail.

Months after the frenzy died down, during an autumn festival in Central Park, disaster struck. It was as if Wally knew he was being hunted and had stayed hidden. Now that the danger for him had passed, he struck with a vengeance. Wally reportedly waited until sundown that fateful day and then slowly slipped out of the sewers and crept up on an unsuspecting family of five.

This was before the age of "take a picture instead of help," so there was no footage of the tragedy. When Wally attacked, panic filled the park. Due to the recent search for Wally, there were still many police departments that had dart guns ready just for him. Though the family could not be saved, Wally was subdued and carted off to Bruce's Alligator Farm.

Bruce reported all traces of the story were covered up by the city of New York. It was a blight in their history they wanted forgotten. Pretty sure Bruce was full of crap and caught him in the swamp.

Chapter 20: Time

We remained isolated in the compound for the next week. We gave up trying to use the television and stayed in contact with the outside world through the shortwave radio. Bruce had a small network of survivalists and prepper friends he kept in communication with. Some of the main connections of the network were Crazy Tom and Paranoid Billy. We did not use the first part of their names when we addressed them. The first parts just seemed to fit them well, but they were our lifeline to the world. In hindsight, we should have been more selective.

Crazy Tom told us that he had heard all major cities and most minor cities had fallen into chaos and zombies ruled the land. Those not killed by zombies were being ravaged by the flu. Crazy Tom told us he had heard that the zombies were possibly caused by the flu or some new designer drug. Regardless of how it started, Crazy Tom informed us it could be spread by a bite from the infected. Of course, the only way to stop an infected person was to destroy the brain. Glad I shot Pantless Zombie Guy in the head! Crazy Tom said he was holed up in his bunker and had food and water for a year. We promised to maintain contact every Saturday and listen in every day between 8:00 pm and 8:10 pm for emergencies. Crazy Tom closed by saying, "Talk to Crazy Billy, he may have more information."

"You're Crazy, Billy is Paranoid," Bruce informed Crazy Tom.

"Yep, Crazy Billy sure is paranoid, over and out," were Tom's closing words.

Paranoid Billy lived in an undisclosed area deep in the Florida woods. He reported they were isolated and planned on keeping it that way. Paranoid Billy reported picking up chatter on his radio that these events were worldwide. He had heard that the EMP affected the entire planet. The reports of rioting and the flu were coming in from everywhere. He stated that his "group" was well prepared and was not accepting visitors. Paranoid Billy said, "We should all keep in contact with Paranoid Tom weekly."

Bruce responded, "You're Paranoid Billy, Tom's Crazy."

"Tom might be a little crazy, but his being paranoid may just keep us all safe, over and out," was Paranoid Billy's parting statement.

We settled into a routine and gave up on regular radio and television after the first week. We exclusively relied on the prepper network to keep us informed of the goings-on of the outside world. Probably not the best idea to listen to a bunch of paranoid isolationists who were just waiting for the breakdown of society, a plague, or zombie apocalypse.

I biked to our home every day and fed the animals and checked our property. Every now and then I would catch sight of a hippie walking in the distance but never made contact. I moved quickly on the bike. I would get to our house and look for signs of entry. The dogs patrolled the yard and protected the chickens and goats. I would return with fresh eggs and milk every day.

Monday of the second week, Crazy Tom made contact at 8:00 pm that evening. Tom reported he had heard that New York, London, and Cairo had all fallen to the zombie hordes. Tom reported that he had heard from Crazy Pete that this was reliable. Warning signs should come up when a crazy person calls someone crazy.

We were trying to resign ourselves to living in the new zombie apocalypse world. We discussed plans for going into town and seeing what remained of civilization. We wanted to protect the kids as much as possible from this terrible new reality. We were discussing plans for travelling to town when we heard a banging and a voice coming from the direction of the front gate.

We jumped into our roles. Bruce went to the tower, but not before reminding me to keep my finger off the trigger. I gave him a different finger in response. Spirit went to the tower with Bruce. They seemed to be hitting it off well, though moving slowly. Cathy and I went cautiously, again, to the front gate, rifles in hand.

Chapter 21: Holy Moly

I climbed the front gate and looked down and saw a man in priest's robes gently tapping a staff on the main gate. This was the first person we had seen since the Pantless Poncho Zombie Guy. "Hiya, preacher dude," was the best I came up with. I should have said something more fitting of the situation, like, "Well met, fair traveler, friend or foe?" Nope, "Hiya, preacher dude." He looked up a bit confused and with a brief look of disdain.

He quickly recovered and said, "Well met, my good man, I seek refuge." Damn it, but at least I had a chance to redeem myself with a classy response.

"Uh, okay," I replied.

Right after my great rebuttal, Bruce radioed in, "Riggs to Weiner, sitrep please," loud enough for the preacher dude to hear. This was followed by a loud snort by Cathy, also heard by the preacher dude. I sighed heavily and almost leaned back on the gate. Instead, I responded, "Wheeler to Riggs, visitor at gate, seems normal and friendly." Oh, "sitrep" is military talk for "situation report."

Bruce stated, "Riggs to Weiner, search him while Huckleberry covers." Followed by another snort from inside the gate.

"Damn it, will do, over and out." and I switched off my radio. Not my best first impression. The preacher looked up at me with startlingly piercing blue eyes. He looked to be in his late fifties and in good shape. His staff also looked quite stout and would make a good club.

"Lower your staff and bag preacher dude," I politely told the priest.

"Don't call me preacher dude, young man," the priest lashed out sharply. Considering he had come to our door seeking help, his temper flare-up seemed out of place. However, I was more focused on being called "young man." Since I had hit my forties, I had been sensitive about my age, and the good priest calling me "young man" earned him points in my book. Sure, he seemed a bit off and way too intense and volatile for a priest of his age.

The priest did as instructed. I came off the wall and opened the gate with Cathy covering me. The priest raised his hands and said, "No need to be alarmed, I am unarmed and mean you no harm." I frisked him and allowed him to pick up his staff and bag and enter the gate under Cathy's watchful eyes.

We walked to the visitor center and met Spirit and Bruce at the front door. The kids were confined to the tower until we could screen the newcomer. Bruce seemed to know of our guest and asked, "Aren't you the guy that runs that cult outside of Stoneburg?"

"It is not a cult, young man, and yes, that was my church until yesterday when my flock went astray." It did not go unnoticed that he called Bruce "young man" also, and he looked a lot older than me.

"Didn't you rewrite the Bible or something?" Bruce inquired.

"I merely polished His work and made a few corrections."

Spirit had been quiet and had been hanging back until this point, "Pretty sure you aren't allowed to do that."

The priest looked at Spirit with obvious contempt and said, "What would you know of the Bible and church? Looks like you could use some time in church, young lady."

It was official, the preacher dude was an ass. And he uses the word "young" indiscriminately. "Let's all calm down and let the preacher get cleaned up," I suggested.

"Priest," he corrected me, "and my apologies. It has been a long few days for me, and I have been spread thin. I have let my tired body influence my tongue. Please forgive me, young lady. My name is Father Roger E. Morgore."

Bruce showed Father Roger to the restrooms and gave him a change of clothes.

With the priest gone, we discussed his addition to the group. "I don't like him," both Cathy and Spirit said at the same time.

"And his name sounds made up, almost as if there is something more to it. Roger E. Morgore?" Cathy added.

"Well, the guns are all secured other than what we have at the ready, so keep your guns secure and lock your doors at night. He can sleep on the couch in the visitor center for now," said Bruce.

"He can have my room, I will stay with the kids if that is alright with Cathy and Jack," Spirit said.

"I don't think the preacher dude would take to your room, Spirit. Cathy and I will move to your room, you and the kids take ours. The preacher can have the kids' room." I am really good at problem solving.

We went up to switch rooms. Just as Cathy and I finished moving into the 1970's deluxe love suite, Father Roger walked by, stopped, peered into our room, looked me in the eye, shook his head, and walked away. "Damn it," I said as Cathy gave yet another snort.

At dinner, things seemed to have calmed down greatly. Father Roger seemed to have improved his view of Spirit. In fact, he seemed to be viewing Spirit a lot during the dinner. We told Father Roger a brief version of our story, leaving out the untimely demise of Pantless Poncho Zombie Guy. We then sat back to hear Father Roger's story.

"As some of you are aware, I founded the Church of the Pathetic Souls in Stoneburg twenty-eight years ago. We had a congregation of seventy-seven at our height and were at twenty-three when my parishioners turned from me, I mean from the word."

We urged the priest to continue. Brie and Colby were bored, so we sent them up to the watchtower with slingshots and metal ball bearings. They were also given a radio and told to call in if they saw anything out of the ordinary.

Father Roger went on to tell us that he gathered his flock at the church a few weeks ago when the world started to crumble. He reported they finally locked themselves into the church grounds when all communications were lost, the power went out, and most of the cars died. They had a good amount of food and were isolated enough that unless someone intentionally sought them out, they would be left alone.

The priest informed us they were a peaceful group and had no weapons to speak of. He reported that as time went on and cabin fever set in, tempers and accusations began to flare. The preacher said his flock was being tested, and "alas, they failed," turning on him and driving him out of his own church. He was unclear as to what reason they gave to banish him.

"No offense meant, Father Roger, but we always heard that the Church of the Pathetic Souls was a doomsday cult. Planning for a zombie apocalypse or end of the world," Bruce tactfully stated.

I was waiting for a "young man" response, but the food and a glass of wine seemed to have made the priest much more cordial. "We were preparing for the coming End of Days until my flock went astray," he answered with a sad, distant look.

Pretty sure Father Roger was a looney. At least he had become less intense, though his excessive eye contact with Spirit seemed to make her nervous. It also seemed to annoy Bruce.

After supper, Bruce brought out another bottle of wine and some fancy cheeses. Father Roger informed us that, "I'm a cheese connoisseur. It is one of God's wonderful gifts to mankind." He smiled and took some slices and filled his cup of wine.

I knew he was a bad apple. Most cheese nuts are, I have come to learn. I asked Father Roger if he knew how to shoot a gun.

"Heaven's no. I leave that up to those of a lower station than I." The preacher sure wasn't good at making friends. Anyone who followed him was, well, a pathetic soul for sure. Quite sure we needed to ditch him when the opportunity arose.

The rest of the group stared at him in disbelief. Bruce had his mouth hanging open in shock. Cathy was smiling slightly and barely shaking her head. Spirit just stared silently. This was turning out to be one heck of a party.

"Time for bed. Who has the first watch?" I asked.

Father Roger did not volunteer to help, and I am quite sure no one would trust him on watch. We went to our assigned locations, and those going to bed locked their bedroom doors.

Chapter 23: Status

The next morning, we all got up and began doing various chores. The kids were in the watchtower keeping a lookout. Spirit and Bruce were feeding the alligators. Cathy was cleaning the living area. I was preparing to dash off to our house to collect some eggs and goat milk. I would also check the area and feed the animals. Father Roger had not yet made an appearance by the time I left.

When I returned an hour later. Bruce, Cathy, and Spirit were in the visitor center lobby, obviously agitated. I inquired what was wrong.

"That son of a gun has been making demands of us all day as if we are his servants. And if he stares at Spirit any harder, she will burst into flames. Is it wrong to want to kick a priest's butt? I won't go to hell for just wanting to, right?" Bruce spat out.

"Pretty sure he isn't a real priest," Spirit observed.

"Good, I can kick a fake priest's butt and not go to hell. I am pretty sure," Bruce smiled.

"No one is kicking anyone's butt. Right, Cathy?" I said.

"He told me to draw his bath water and fetch him some lunch, I vote to kick the fake priest's butt," Cathy, the voice of reason, stated.

We were interrupted by footsteps coming from the stairs. Everyone became silent and stared in the direction of the disturbance. A moment later Father Roger entered our view, wearing my robe and slippers.

"Ah, you're back. Oh good. Are those fresh eggs? Bruce, you're a good enough cook, how about you make us a second breakfast?" Father Roger requested.

Now I am quite sure my robe and slippers were in our room when I left this morning. I am pretty darn sure Cathy did not lend him my favorite robe also. At this point I was mildly annoyed. Cathy seemed to notice my state and said, "Don't."

Too late. I walked up to the fake priest and grabbed him by the collar of my beloved robe. To his weak resistance and futile pleas to be "released" I drug him outside. The rest of the group followed excitedly. I brought him to Wally's enclosure.

"This is Wally's room. No one is allowed in Wally's room without permission. Do you understand?" I asked.

The fake priest silently nodded his head vigorously.

"If you ever enter mine, or anyone else's room without permission, and use their favorite robe and slippers without permission, then I will give you permission to enter Wally's room." This seemed to confuse everyone, including the priest.

"But I don't want permission to enter Wally's room," the priest stuttered.

"That would ruin your robe and slippers for sure," Bruce added.

Hey, I was mad and flaked a bit. I was usually good under pressure and also quite the wordsmith. Since I had everyone's attention, I closed with. "Shut up. If you keep acting like a jerk, we will kick you out of here."

"Okay, so Wally has nothing to do with this, right?" Asked the priest.

The tension was broken by a call from Colby, "Little Cheese to Weiner, strangers approaching gate, over."

"Little Cheese? And you're grounded," I replied.

"Grounded from what, over?" came the quick rebuttal.

Damn it. "Bruce is heading up with Spirit, and Father Roger, Cathy, and I are heading to the gate."

Chapter 24: Pathetic Souls At The Gate

As Cathy and I approached the gate, we heard talking from the other side. Not zombies, I guessed. We both climbed up to the catwalk and looked down on a group of men and women dressed in brown robes. We noticed that many were carrying staffs.

"Uh, can I help you?" I tried to speak with authority, but my voice decided to crack at that moment, which made me sound as if I was just reaching puberty. Cathy helped by snort laughing.

"We seek the priest," replied a voice that was deep and did not crack.

"Riggs to Weiner, sitrep?" Bruce chimed in unhelpingly. Unhelpingly may be a made-up word, but it fits perfectly here. Cathy snorted again, unhelpingly.

Annoyed, I responded, "Pathetic Souls at the gate, over and out." I then turned off my radio.

Deep-voiced fella, who also happened to be holding a staff, spoke again in his authoritative voice, "We seek the priest. We demand you release him to us if he is in your care."

Now I try to be polite, especially when visiting someone else's property. They were pretty demanding for visitors armed with sticks. That and then hearing my call sign had agitated me greatly. So, I responded, "Did you bring a gift?" I asked in my friendliest voice.

Most of the robed-clad group appeared confused and looked at each other as if searching for a proper response to the question. The deep-voiced fellow finally came up with, "What do you mean, did we bring a gift?"

"Exactly what I said. Did you bring us a nice gift?"

"I don't understand, why would we bring a gift?" The deep-voiced fellow responded as his cohorts milled about with confusion growing.

"Most people bring gifts when they visit their neighbors for the first time," I educated the rude trespassers.

The deep-voiced fella responded, "Is there someone else up there we can talk to?" That was a great setup from a great movie, it was a line in the script from Monty Python's Holy Grail.

I gave the visitors the proper response, "No, now go away or I shall taunt you a second time!" That seemed to greatly agitate the speaker and most of his entourage.

"If you have him, we demand you turn him over to us immediately," deep voice said.

"There are multiple rifles pointed at you and your friends. If you try to enter, we will fire," I informed the robed mob. Cathy conveyed this turn of events to Bruce via radio.

"Why do you want him so bad?" I inquired.

One of the visitors spoke up, saying, "He tried to seduce my wife."

Another robed man said the same had happened with his wife.

Another fellow spoke, saying, "He seduced my grandmother."

"Listen, him flirting with your wives is no reason to hunt him down. Were your wives actually seduced by him?" I asked.

The two husbands both responded, "No."

Unfortunately, the guy with the grandmother did not respond "no." I noticed one of the older ladies in the crowd had a big cheesy grin on her face. She did not present as a victim, but having a religious leader seduce grandma would piss me off too.

"What are you going to do with him if we turn him over to you?" I wasn't very fond of the priest, but I wasn't about to turn someone over to an angry mob. Sure, he was a jerk, but I would rather just send him on his way.

"We will hold a trial and sentence him as we see fit," the leader responded.

"Don't you mean if you find him guilty, you will sentence him?" I asked without expecting an answer.

"We do not plan on leaving here without him."

"Get comfortable then. Touch any part of this gate and we will defend it with extreme prejudice." I heard the term "extreme prejudice" in a movie and always wanted to use it. It means to do something mercilessly, which did not really fit with our group, but the Pathetic Souls did not know that.

We set a guard to watch them. All the adults, except the priest, took a turn. The church group made three campfires in the parking lot and seemed to try and get comfortable as night approached. They appeared to be well behaved as far as angry mobs go.

Chapter 25: Strangers In The Dark

The visitors sent a group to the church earlier in the day and brought back supplies. They were not overly festive, but their food preparation and chatter over the campfires were a bit noisy. They exhibited no hostile behavior and seemed to take the approach that they would just wait us out.

Around midnight, Spirit radioed in that there was "something happening, and we better get down here." Bruce went to the tower with Father Roger. The kids were woken up and told to stay alert, and Cathy and I ran to the gate with our rifles in hand.

We climbed up and joined Spirit at the top of the gate. The group of Pathetic Souls clustered together and faced the woods to the north of the parking lot. They had grown silent, and a large amount of noise was coming from the woods and sounded like it was headed their way. It sounded like a small army was trudging through the swampy forest.

"What the hell is going on, Spirt?" I asked nervously.

"The heck if I know, and its Spirit," was her nonhelpful response.

We readied our weapons on the gate and watched anxiously. The Pathetic Souls had their staffs out and were shuffling their feet in anticipation. No one said a word as we waited for the arrival of the unseen noisemakers.

Finally, a couple of hippies broke through the tree line, followed by about ten more. They must have been wandering the woods for days and were attracted to the noise, fires, and food. They looked very disheveled and very hungry. They were making growling sounds and, yes, walking like zombies on a mission.

The Pathetic Souls saw the abominations dressed in tie-dye coming at them and took flight. They ran down the driveway screaming in fright. The hippies (zombies?) slowly following them.

"Well, that was unexpected," I told Cathy and Spirit.

"Riggs to Huckleberry, did the hippie army just chase the Jesus Freaks away?" Bruce asked.

"Yes, and I don't think you are allowed to say Jesus Freaks," responded Cathy.

"That was freaking cool!" observed Spirit excitedly. "I saw Sleepy Bob with them. Boy, did he look bad." The zombies looked like they had not eaten much and were covered in leaves and dirt. The parking lot was silent with only the campfires burning. I had Spirit and Cathy cover me while I put out the fires.

When I returned to the gate, Father Roger had joined the group and seemed very excited. "Those lost souls chased off my would-be abductors. They must be the true chosen ones."

"I don't think so, Tex," I told the priest.

Apparently, the nickname "Tex" is offensive to priests, or at least to Father Roger. His piercing blue eye focused on me with obvious rage, "How dare you disrespect a man of the cloth. You are a fool and will perish with your brethren. I bid you all adieu. I will seek out my new flock."

"Now, Father, I didn't..." was all I got out before Cathy chimed in.

"Well, get the flock out of here, and good luck with those new friends of yours," Cathy stated, holding her rifle at the low ready. The priest "huffed" and walked out the gate in search of his new flock.

We left Spirit at the gate to finish her watch and returned to the visitor center. We filled Bruce and the kids in with the new turn of events. They all responded, "Good." The preacher did not make a good impression on my "brethren," I supposed.

"Get the flock out of here," Brie repeated, "Good one, Cathy." Children were so easy to impress.

Chapter 26: Unexpected Pest

Cathy and I slept in after all the drama from the night before. I got up and headed to the kitchen for coffee and food. When I entered the kitchen, I found Colby, Brie, and Spirit all in the kitchen with alcohol swabs, broken pens, and needles spread out on the table. Spirit had a tank top on, and the kids were looking at her tattoo, discussing how to spell "Spirit." This can't be good, I thought to myself. Oops, I said that out loud. They all looked up, Brie and Colby with smiles, and Spirit with an "oh crap" look.

"What the heck are you knuckleheads doing?" I politely asked.

"Fixing Spirit's tattoo." Not sure which knucklehead said that, as I was busy shaking my head at Spirit.

"You thought this was a good idea?"

"They talked me into it."

"So, the 10-year-olds are the brains of this operation?" I asked with much exasperation.

Thankfully we were interrupted by Bruce calling on the radio, "Car slowly approaching front gate."

"Say again. Did you say car?" I asked.

"Roger that. Red Mustang, looks like a 1965 fastback."

Oh crap.

"Did you say red Mustang?" Cathy radioed in with an excited voice.

"Roger that. Positions everyone," Bruce demanded

With a heavy heart I met Cathy at the front door and made our way to the front gate. I had to move fast to keep up with Cathy, who could hardly contain her excitement.

By the time we reached the top of the catwalk, the Mustang had pulled up in front of the gate, and the engine was off. The older cars were not affected by the EMP since they had no fragile computer components. I had always planned on getting an older truck but always ended up spending the money on something else.

Both doors on the Mustang opened, and I raised my rifle slightly. "Knock it off!" Cathy snapped, and I lowered the gun.

From the driver's side, out stepped an attractive 42-year-old black lady with an athletic build and intelligent green eyes. She wore a devilish smile and said, "Hi Cathy, hi Idiot."

"Hey, fu..." a smack to the back of my head stopped my response.

Cathy snorted, the newcomer snorted.

"Hi Steele," I said to the handsome blond fellow that exited from the passenger seat. Sandra had been Cathy's best friend since college. She was a lawyer, was wickedly smart, and ran marathons for fun. Her faithful companion, John Steele, was also athletic, dashingly handsome, and had a tough guy name too. Who runs marathons for fun?

"Riggs to Weiner, sitrep?" lots of snort laughs followed Bruce's request. I really need to remember to address that call sign before it sticks.

"Visitors are friendlies, escorting them in. Bringing the car in also."

Sandra and I seemed to have a love-hate relationship. She loved to hate me. She did seem to know that I adored Cathy and was 100 percent committed to her. She even seemed to realize that Cathy and I were happy together. She appeared to really like the kids. She just loved to hate me in a playful, mean, hurtful way…

Cathy and I had no idea what Steele did for a living, but we suspected he did nothing for a living. He was financially secure somehow. He went by "Steele" which just pissed me off.

Sandra and Steele were escorted to the visitor center. They had met Bruce in the past and got along well. We introduced them to Spirit and walked them upstairs. We had decided that Father Roger would probably not be returning and gave them his room. Unfortunately, in Cathy's haste to get to the front gate, she left our room door wide open. As Sandra and Steel walked by the 70s love room, Sandra stopped, looked in our room, looked at me, and shook her head, then continued to follow Cathy.

After they got settled and cleaned up, they joined us in the dining room. We told them of our recent experiences in detail, except we left out Pantless Poncho Zombie Guy. I sent the kids to the watchtower to keep an eye out. We then settled back over a few glasses of wine to hear their story.

Sandra reported they were at their condo in Tallahassee when the EMP struck. The flu had already hit the town quite hard, so they had been isolating as much as possible. As soon as they realized that the power was not coming back on, they filled every container they had with water, including the bathtub. They also had a small hot tub full of water. Sandra and Steele had spent enough time around me and knew that eight drops of regular bleach placed in a gallon of water will make it safe for consumption after 30 minutes. Dirtier water may require more bleach.

They cooked all their refrigerated and frozen food as soon as they could, using their grill on their second-floor deck. Grilling on a balcony is a terrible idea, but they had little choice, I guess. They then turned to their dry goods. A little over a week later they were low on food. The neighbors and others kept going from door to door looking for food and water. They seemed to get more aggressive by the hour.

They also noted the strange behavior occurring on the street outside their condo. Stores, and some dwellings, were being broken into. There were numerous fights or disturbances on the streets. They also noticed more and more people walking around in a daze and attacking people unprovoked. They decided enough was enough. They loaded up the Mustang, grabbed their go bags, and headed our way.

Prepper educational moment here. A "go bag" is a backpack or duffle bag full of emergency supplies. It is prepacked and ready to go in a moment's notice. It should be light enough to carry long distances, as motorized vehicles may not be an option. It should contain at least a three-day supply of food and water, a change of clothes, a flashlight, fire-making equipment, a knife, a multi-tool, a first aid kit, a hand-cranked radio, hand sanitizer, an emergency blanket, medications, and copies of personal papers that may be needed. There are more items you can add as you see fit. I ditched the change of clothes and added room for ammo. I also always have a rifle and handgun ready. I recommend an AR that takes 5.56 NATO ammo and a 9mm handgun. These are among the most commonly used rounds and make it easier to find additional ammo. Oh, gum comes in handy too.

The trip to our place from Tallahassee is usually an 11-hour ride. The trip took them 4 days of slow travel by day. They took the back roads, which were clogged with abandoned, broken-down cars. There were also many people on the roads closer to the towns. They tried to avoid the larger cities since they saw what was beginning to happen in Tallahassee. They would look for secluded places to park for the night and kept watch with their guns out in plain view to deter inquisitive visitors. Having the guns in sight could also attract those looking for guns to take from others, so they kept a sharp eye out for people sneaking up on them. They made it a point to stay down or under cover when possible.

On multiple occasions they ran into hungry groups or the "zombie people" and had to speed off or reverse course. Before finally reaching our house, they had to fire their guns on three occasions. They reported they did not have to shoot anyone and just shot as warnings. This breaks the" rules of a gunfight," but I will tell you about those later since I don't want to feed you too many educational moments at once.

Sandra reported that when they got close to our house, they had to turn around a few times because our mailbox was missing, and the driveway was hidden. After about their third turnaround. "Some zoned-out zombie dude in a dress shirt and tie exited the woods and stepped in front of our car. We pulled to a stop about thirty feet from him. We noticed he had blood on his shirt and a perfect shoe print on the center of his shirt."

It was good to know my neighbor Robert was still patrolling around our property. Sandra continued, "Steele got out of the car, and after he made sure the guy was not cooperative or coherent, he added his own shoeprint to his chest and sent the guy back into the woods. Steele turned to get back in the car and noticed your hidden driveway."

"We parked the car on the side of the road and were trying to figure out how to get around your electric fence and make contact with you without getting shot. Our radio was destroyed by the EMP, so we had no way of calling you. Honking repeatedly seemed like a bad idea. We heard a vehicle coming down the road, so we waited with our guns in hand on the other side of the Mustang. Your neighbor, Gilbert, pulled up on his old four-wheeler and said you were with Bruce." They had met Gilbert, Jane, and Timmy on occasion while visiting us.

"We started to make our way to the alligator farm. There was a lot of activity in the woods. We saw a pack of hippies stumbling around as if following someone. We also saw about 15 or 20 motorcycle riders off in the distance riding down the highway," Sandra stated.

I asked more about the motorcycle group, but they were too distant for them to have details. We allowed Sandra and Steele to rest before adding them to the guard rotation. We called the kids down and forbade them to tattoo anyone, including themselves, and sent them to bed and Bruce to the watchtower.

Chapter 28: Time Passes

With more people to help with chores and watches, we had time to communicate with others via shortwave radio. We heard various reports from strangers all over the USA. Most of the time we monitored but did not engage in conversation. Some of the chatter got strange. There were increased sightings of UFOs and Bigfoot. Though some of the reports were from credible sources, we laughed them off.

Crazy Tom informed us some of his neighbors came by and told him that the small town he lived close to had completely shut down. No one came out, and the police had either abandoned their post or were dead. He was told that drug-crazed lunatics ran the streets, and no one was safe. Sounded like zombies to us, and Crazy Tom agreed.

Crazy Tom reported that his house was separate from his bunker, and few people knew about his well-hidden bunker. Tom informed us that he had strung up new cameras he had stored in his Faraday chamber. Man, how does everyone have a Faraday chamber but me? At least I had a Faraday box. He reported seeing small groups and families walking the roads during the day. He noted that most of those groups were armed with guns. He also saw strange groups of wanderers shambling along both day and night. Crazy Tom also said he saw a group of about twenty-five motorcycle riders pass by on the highway. Though Tom was quite far from us, it could be the same group of bikers seen around here.

A couple of days after Sandra and Steele arrived, a small group of travelers turned down the driveway to the alligator farm. Three men, two women, a teenager, and two children around 6 years old walked to our gate. Two of the men and one of the women carried hunting rifles, but they were strung on their backs. The two men walked to the front of the gate, where Cathy told them to halt and state their business.

One of the men said his name was Ronald and asked to speak with Bruce. Cathy called for Bruce to come to the gate. Sandra was covering Cathy from the watchtower with her sniper rifle and made this obvious to the newcomers.

Bruce arrived and said, "Ronald, what are you doing out of Dixon City? Is that your son and his family?"

Ronald replied, "We had to leave Dixon, it was starting to be overrun with dangerous characters. This is Ronnie Junior, his wife Tonya, their three kids and Harold, Tonya's father. We are headed to my cabin by Lakeville. Can we stay the night here? We will move along in the morning."

Bruce said he had to discuss it with the group, but to sit down and relax out front. We met in the kitchen of the visitor center. Bruce vouched for Ronald and Ronnie Junior and felt that the rest were safe to trust based on his friendship with Ronald. It was agreed upon that they would be allowed to stay the night and given provisions to ensure their safe arrival at their destination.

They were ushered in and given access to the showers and restrooms. We then sat down to a good dinner. It was Steele's turn at the front gate, and the kids were in the tower. I was eager to learn what was happening at Dixon City since I had had run-ins with a couple of people there.

Ronald informed us there was always a pretty good population of lowlifes in Dixon City. He reported that the police were still maintaining a vague sense of control in some of the better neighborhoods, but the rougher neighborhoods seemed to have large numbers of dangerous people milling about at all hours of the day, and attacks were up drastically. Ronald had a cabin by a lake that was outfitted and secluded. They planned on staying there for the time being.

Bruce asked if the three hunting rifles they carried were all they had for defense. They informed us they had two 9mm handguns also. After some discussion, we decided to give them an AR-15 to borrow with 300 rounds of ammunition. Ronald must have been a good friend for Bruce to do that.

We exchanged as much information as both groups could think to share. We told them of our adventures to date, of course leaving out Pantless Poncho Zombie Guy. They had not seen any strange lights in the sky, but they all reported seeing strange things in the woods.

The next morning, we shored up their supplies and added an AR-15 to their defenses. I walked them as far as the road that my house was on, and after they continued on, I checked my house and animals and returned to the alligator farm.

Chapter 29: Sights Unseen

When I returned, Bruce was at the gate. He let me in, but I sensed something was wrong. "Out with it, Bruce, what's wrong?" I asked. Bruce was pale and looked dazed.

"I saw something while I was on watch," was all Bruce said.

"What did you see, Bruce?" I inquired, slightly anxious.

"I'm not sure what I saw," was Bruce's too short answer.

"Bruce, for goodness sakes, tell me what you saw."

"It was about halfway between the highway and the parking lot. It crossed the driveway slowly. It stopped in the middle of the driveway, turned and looked at me, then continued across the rest of the driveway and into the woods," Bruce said in a hushed voice.

"What did it look like?" I asked.

"Jack, it was about seven feet tall and covered in hair. It wasn't wearing clothes, unless it was wearing a fur coat in the middle of summer in Florida," was Bruce's almost reverent response. He cleared his throat, but said nothing more.

Now when I was a younger man, for fun I would tie large cutout footprints to my shoes, and I would stomp around the paths and trails of Florida leaving fake Bigfoot prints for others to find. I figured a good hoax was harmless fun and added a little excitement in someone's life.

I would also buy glow sticks, helium tanks, and balloons to release fake UFOs. I would wait until a nice summer night and drive to the outskirts of town and send glow sticks attached to balloons into the night sky. The next morning, I scanned the internet looking for Bigfoot tracks or UFO sightings. Pretty sure that if there were people still doing that, they would stop for the moment. I stopped doing the balloon releases because the plastic and latex were bad for the wildlife. I also grew up a bit.

I figured Bruce was just stir crazy, so I suggested he go with me to recheck on mine and Cathy's houses and feed the animals. He was hesitant to leave the safety of the compound after seeing the creature, but soon agreed he needed to get out for a while.

We prepared to go and were on our way within half an hour. Not many, if anyone but us, used the trail from the alligator farm to our house, so we did not run into anyone, though the odd noises were a regular occurrence on most of the trips there and back.

We made it to my property and rechecked the perimeter, fed the animals, and collected any eggs that were there since my earlier visit today. We entered the house and took a break, having a beer from my fridge. Solar power is great. We decided to raid the pantry and found a large jar of gummy bears in the back of "Cathy's Only" snack cabinet. I was deeply hurt that she would hide such a treasure from me and the kids since we usually shared this type of treat. Usually the "Cathy Only" snacks were not snacks I and the kids wanted anyway. Who likes rice cakes?

They seemed a bit old, and the jar wasn't that big, so Bruce and I ate all of them. We finished our beers, had some beef jerky, and were on our way home after a few minutes.

About halfway back, both mine and Bruce's stomachs started making noticeably loud sounds. About five minutes out from the alligator farm, both of us began to feel very bloated and gaseous. We made it to the compound and were both sick to our stomachs and suffering from horrific diarrhea.

Sandra was manning the gate, and Steele was in the tower. The kids were sent to play video games, and Cathy and Spirit herded us both to the nearest couches. There were often benefits to being with someone who has a medical background, but this was not one of those occasions.

Cathy assumed the bloating and stomach issues were caused by something we ate. She questioned us and soon discovered our eating the gummies she had in her cabinet. Cathy was a very responsible lady, so I knew they were not THC (marijuana-infused) gummies. She would never use them, and she would never allow them around the kids.

This is another educational moment, but not for preppers, just for the common good of mankind. There was once a famous gummy bear company that decided to make a sugar-free gummy bear treat using maltitol. Now maltitol has a rather dramatic effect on many people, especially when your body is not used to it, and you use large amounts of it. The famous gummy bear company stopped making them after notoriously hilarious reviews were left on a popular online seller site. Though the product is no longer produced, the hilarious reviews are still out there, haunting the World Wide Web, and are worth seeking out. Be warned, other companies still make sugar-free gummy bears using maltitol.

After Cathy finished laughing, she informed us that she hid them so I would not eat them and meant to throw them out. We were confined to the bedrooms and spent the rest of the day in and out of the restrooms. We were also scolded for getting into Cathy's cabinet, and she said her rice cakes better all be there. The rest of the group tried to avoid the second floor that day. The possible Bigfoot sighting was all but forgotten.

Chapter 30: Strange Things

Our stomachs were much better the next day. Bruce and I were still taking it easy while manning the watchtower and drinking our morning coffee. Steele was at the front gate when he called, reporting three armed people were approaching the gate. He reported that their firearms were strapped to their backs, and it appeared to be a group of one female and two tubby males.

When they got to forty feet in front of the gate, Steele ordered them to halt. Bruce and I covered Steele from the tower. I had my scope on one of the males. His nose was bandaged, so it was difficult to see his face, but he looked awfully familiar. After some dialogue between Steele and the group, Steele radioed in requesting me and Bruce come to the front gate.

Sandra and Cathy took our places in the tower. Spirit and the kids went to keep an eye on the back part of the compound. Bruce and I approached with AR-15s at the low ready. We climbed up the catwalk on the gate and looked down at our visitors.

I brought my rifle up immediately and pointed it at the bandaged man. Standing between Bubba and Cleo was Fran. Strange that Fran appeared to have a shotgun strapped to her back also. All three raised their hands, and Steele and Bruce looked very confused but raised their rifles also.

"Step away from the lady now!" I demanded.

Fran said, "Jack, is that you behind that rifle?"

Bubba still had his hands up but broke into a broad smile. Cleo started smiling and giggling.

"What the hell is going on?" I asked my rifle, still aimed at the smiling Bubba.

Bubba responded, "I listened to what you said about not chasing ladies during a power outage and the flu hitting everyone. I got cleaned up, got some flowers, and cut a big wedge of cheese for her and went to her apartment and asked her out."

"It was the cheese that got me," Fran stated.

"I think I'm going to be sick," was all I could think to say.

"Bubba kissed you on the mouth," Cleo added laughing.

Steele looked at me and quietly asked, "Should we shoot them?" I think he was joking.

Bruce asked, "Why did Bubba kiss you?" I had left that part out of my description of events I relayed to the group.

"Where are you going? And you can put your hands down, I think?" I stated.

"Things got worse in town, we lost two buddies, and we saw the zombies you were talking about," Bubba informed us. "We left town and are heading to my uncle Ronnie's and Ronnie Junior's lake house."

"You're kidding," I stated.

Bubba and Cleo looked at each other confused, and Fran just stared up at us smiling.

Bubba finally responded, "Thanks for the cheese, without that and your advice, I would never have gotten to know Fran."

"You can't lay that on me," I said a little too loud. Fran laughed, and the goofballs just stood there smiling. "Just wait there a minute."

I turned to Bruce and Steele, who had bemused looks on their faces. "Should we let them in and feed them? They're obviously going to your friend Ronald's lake house. They are pretty harmless, I think."

Bruce and Steele agreed if they were disarmed, they could come in. Steele said sending them off without some help would be like dumping puppies and a college girl on the side of the road. We offered them food and shelter for the night as long as they gave up their guns while in the compound. They agreed without hesitating. I am shocked they made it this far.

They were escorted in and directed to the restrooms to get cleaned up. After they were presentable, we introduced everyone to them and sat down to lunch. We sent the kids to the tower to keep watch while we settled in to hear their story. Sharp eyed children can be very helpful.

Chapter 31: Drunkards And Fools

Bubba reported that after being struck by the large wheel of cheese, Cleo got him to his house and bandaged his nose. Cleo reported he then went to his home to get the last of his beer to bring back to Bubba's. As he approached his house, he saw his front door was wide open. Since Bubba and he had been planning on hunting earlier that day, he had his shotgun on him. He entered the house and found all his belongings, including his beer, were gone. Heartbroken, he returned to Bubba's house and spent the next day helping him while he recovered from the blow to his head.

The next day Bubba was feeling better. He reported that having a near-death experience made him see things in a new light. Not every man is lucky enough to survive a cheese wheel to the head. He decided to get cleaned up and find the girl that caught his eye. He thought hard about what that stranger said about what not to do when trying to meet a lady.

Cleo and he spent the day looking for Fran and traced her to the apartment building she lived in. Bubba then bathed and trimmed his goatee and brushed and parted his dark brown hair on one side. He put on his best beer shirt and tucked it in.

Now Bubba was not an ugly fellow, but he did not clean up too well either. He was twenty-four years old and a bit overweight. He had a friendly and slightly lost look about him. His buddy, Cleo, looked a lot like him, only larger and with a gap in his teeth.

"When he tucked in his shirt, I knew he was serious," Cleo chimed in.

Bubba went to the front door of the apartment and knocked on the door with flowers and a wedge of cheese in his hand. He had told Cleo to stay at the house, but Bubba caught sight of him across the street hiding in the bushes.

A large dark-skinned man opened the door with a gun pointed at him and demanded he state his business. Bubba responded that he was a tree trimmer. Charlie just stared at him for a few moments and broke out into uncontrolled laughter. Bubba just stood there smiling at the man, still holding his flowers and cheese. Charlie lowered his gun slightly.

"Who are you here to see?" asked Charlie.

"I don't know her name, but she is about my age, really pretty, and fast. She has shoulder-length, curly, dark brown hair," was Bubba's response.

"You're one of the guys that was chasing her a few days ago!" Charlie stated, bringing his gun up again.

"I am, and I didn't mean to frighten her, and I am here to apologize. I only wanted to talk to her, and now I know that was not the right way to do that."

Their conversation was interrupted by footsteps coming from the stairs. A moment later Fran appeared and stopped and took in Charlie and Bubba. Fran never got a good look at the men chasing her and did not know about the cheese wheel to the face, so she was not aware of who the big fellow was.

"Fran, this is one of the fella's you told me about. He said he is here to apologize," Charlie declared.

Fran agreed to talk with him in the lobby if Charlie was nearby. They bonded over a wedge of cheese. They went for a walk and agreed to meet again the next day.

Fran had one parting question, "Why is your friend hiding in the bushes across the street?"

"Oh, he is just protective and did not want to leave me with strangers," Bubba answer.

The next day, under Cleo's protective eye, Bubba took Fran to a nearby public park. Bubba packed the last of his soft drinks and another large hunk of Parmesan cheese and crackers. They spent the day in the park talking and laughing. This warmed Cleo's protective heart.

That night Crystal City erupted into violence and chaos. Bubba was awakened to the sound of screaming and yelling. He jumped out of bed and ran to the living room where Cleo was still fast asleep on the couch. He woke Cleo and grabbed their go bags, shotguns, and all the ammo they had and headed to Fran's apartment. Most gun owners that lived in the country had a go bag.

When they left the house, people were everywhere, which was in stark contrast to the last few weeks. Many people were running in terror, while others were kicking in doors and robbing homes and businesses. There was another group that chilled Bubba and Cleo to their bones. There were a large number of bums, many in blue hoodies, shambling about and grabbing people, just like the zombies the stranger had mentioned.

They dodged the mob members as best they could and stopped by the home of their friends' on the way to Fran's apartment. As they approached their friends' house, they found it was on fire and their friends nowhere to be seen. They continued on to Fran's with heavy hearts.

Her neighborhood was calmer, but there were still more people running around than usual, and groups of armed hooligans were roaming the streets. There were two guards in the lobby of Fran's apartment. Charlie recognized Bubba and the fellow who hid in the bushes. Charlie greeted them and had them wait in the lobby while he got Fran.

Bubba and Cleo presented as intimidating to the casual observer. Both are big, and they were carrying three shotguns between them. Most people steered clear of them. They stood with the other guard as a group of four hooligans approached the front door to the apartment. Their leader put his face up to the front door window to look in on their intended target. He caught sight of the guard, Bubba, and Cleo all staring at him. The leader of the hooligans decided to look for easier targets, and they moved on.

The air outside was beginning to fill with smoke, and the sounds of gunfire could be heard close by. The amount of foot traffic was increasing, but they did not see the zombie people in this neighborhood yet.

Fran came to the lobby with fear on her face. She had been watching the growing chaos from the window of her apartment. She agreed to travel with Bubba and Cleo to Bubba's uncle's lake house on the condition that she be given the extra shotgun. "That's why I brought it," was Bubba's answer.

Charlie warned Bubba he would "come looking for him if Fran came to harm." Bubba informed Charlie they weren't going to Harm, they were going to Lakeville and to look for them there. This seemed to appease Charlie somewhat, and they shook hands and parted with Fran.

Chapter 32: Buck Shot

They took the same route out of town I took a few days ago. The guys knew the trails in the area and were accomplished hunters. They were trudging up the same hill where Bubba took a wheel of cheese to the face when they ran into a group of six undesirables that would best be described as zombies.

Though Bubba and Cleo were somewhat backwards and a bit rough and tumble, neither was particularly mean-spirited, and they weren't the type to look for a fight. Nor did they want to hurt or kill anyone, even a zombie at this point.

Fran's gun was loaded with buckshot shells, Cleo's shotgun was loaded with deer slugs, and Bubba's was loaded with rock salt shells. A rock salt shotgun shell is made to deter deer or intruders without killing them. It was agreed that only Bubba would shoot unless the situation became life threatening.

The group of zombies were ahead of them on the slope and started down the slope towards the trio when they heard Bubba, Fran, and Cleo approaching. Our travelers were much quicker than the zombies, however, the trek up the slope had tired all of them somewhat, so they veered off the road, away from the approaching zombies, while still heading uphill. Unfortunately, they could not travel fast enough, and the zombies intercepted them towards the top of the hill.

Bubba brought up his shotgun to fire at the legs of the slow-moving zombies, but Fran stepped forward and pepper-sprayed the front four shambling goons. Now they didn't know much about zombies other than what they saw on television or read in books. Fran and Bubba informed us that pepper spray did affect the zombies. The four in front stopped walking and started swatting the air and moaning loudly. Our travelers pressed on and were almost past the small horde when one of the two goons that were not pepper sprayed grabbed Fran by the shoulder.

Fran spun around frantically and kept the zombie at arm's length, twisting and turning in the road, as the other non-sprayed zombie approached. Bubba spun around as soon as he heard Fran's cries for help. He saw the back of the zombie completely blocking sight of Fran. He was about twenty feet away from the attack when he raised his shotgun to just below waist level and shot the zombie in the rump with rock salt.

Apparently, zombies are affected by pepper spray and react to pain. The zombie released his grasp on Fran and screamed in pain. Fran ran to Bubba, who wrapped an arm around her and pulled her to the top of the hill while Cleo brought up the rear.

Fran was not a weak or frail lady, but the shock of being grabbed by a seemingly mindless monster shook her. She had not believed me when I mentioned zombies to her earlier in the week, and I couldn't blame her. She took comfort in Bubba's warm, kind, slightly dimwitted embrace. Cleo followed along behind, smiling contently.

Cleo had worried about Bubba ever since his wife left him a few years ago. Cleo felt Bubba was the gentle, sensitive type, not like the rest of their now-scattered group. He worried about the friends they left behind but knew they were more than capable of taking care of themselves.

Cleo's main objective was to get Fran and Bubba safely to Uncle Ronnie's cabin by the lake. Growing up, Ronnie always took Bubba and him on camping/fishing trips to the cabin, and Cleo was considered family. He also knew Ronnie and Ronnie Junior were tough as nails and would help them survive whatever was going on.

They pressed on for a few more hours and hit the trails that few others knew about. They found a secluded patch of woods a few yards from the trail and bedded down for the night. Fran had recovered her composure and was back to tough as nails. They took turns guarding all night and made it to dawn without further incident.

They broke camp at first light and continued on their way. They went around Dixon City. They passed by a barn close to the trail with a freshly painted sign saying, "Trespassers will be Shot. Survivors will be Shot Again." The travelers gave the structure wide berth. They had a few encounters with others on the path but heard them in time to hide in the woods and let them pass by. They knew about the alligator farm and decided to stop and see if anyone was there.

Chapter 33: The Bonding

We listened to their story and told them ours, leaving out a few parts that were better off not shared. We then brought out a twelve-pack of one of our most treasured supplies, beer. Both Bubba and Cleo wept openly. Fran tried to console them both while the rest of us watched amused.

A few beers later, Bruce asked if Cleo and Bubba were good hunters. Both affirmed that they were accomplished hunters and would love to help. Bruce said he had plenty of fishing nets set up in the streams that filled the swamps. He reported that this kept his alligators fed, but sometimes they wanted a change, and a few deer would be good for the humans and the alligators. Bruce, Bubba, and Cleo agreed to go hunting tomorrow morning.

Cathy and I pulled Fran aside while they were making plans and made sure she was not being held against her will or had been brainwashed. She assured us that she was happy, and Bubba was a drastic change from the last drug-dealing jerk she dated. She thanked me for bringing them together. I demanded she not give me credit for that.

We went to bed early that day, and true to their word, the three hunters got up at 4:00 am and took off in Bruce's old pickup armed with a rifle and two shotguns. They were gone a couple of hours when they returned in a flurry of panic.

Bruce reported they had shot a large buck, field dressed him and placed him in the back of the old pickup truck. As they were shutting the tailgate, the hippie zombies stumbled onto them, and one of them bit Bubba on the arm before they could react. Bruce shoved the attacking zombie aside, and they jumped into the truck and drove straight back to the compound.

Cleo was crying uncontrollably, and Bubba was in shock, staring off into space. Bruce, though upset, took charge of the situation. Bruce instructed Bubba to be handcuffed and requested Cathy clean and dress the wound. Fran became hysterical and demanded to know why Bubba had to be handcuffed.

"In case he turns into a zombie, he will be less likely to hurt us before we can contain him," Bruce explained.

Cleo started crying louder, Cathy rushed off to get the first aid kit. Bruce turned to Spirit and told her where the handcuffs were and not to bring the ones with pink fur on them. Did he say pink fur?

Fran started screaming and begging us to save Bubba. I told her to calm down and we would do all that we could.

"After I left Lonny, I thought I would be alone forever," cried Fran.

"Lonny from Dixon City?" I asked right before Cathy smacked the back of my head and told me to focus. Steele took the kids to the truck to deal with the deer and distract Brie and Colby from the terror at hand.

Bubba was lying down on a couch and said he was feeling dizzy. His wound was cleaned and dressed, and he was handcuffed for our safety. The wound was not deep, and had it not been a bite from a zombie, it would have hardly been worth worrying about. For such a small, seemingly insignificant wound, we were terrified. Cathy gave him a dose of penicillin just in case.

We all sat in the lobby watching and waiting. Bruce, Cathy, Sandra, and I all had our pistols on us. About three hours later, Bubba reported that he was having trouble breathing and he felt hot. He began to breathe heavily. He broke out into a sweat and started to get fidgety.

"I think this is the end, I can feel it in my veins. I am sorry I met you so late, Fran, I know you were my one true love. There is a sharp pain in my back. Please help me!" Bubba pleaded, panicking.

Cleo got up and held the weeping Fran gently. He whispered comforting words to her, asking her to be strong for Bubba.

Cathy took Bubba's vitals. His temperature was normal, his blood pressure was surprisingly good, and his oxygen levels were excellent. He did appear to be hyperventilating a bit though.

Cathy had Bubba roll over, and we discovered he was lying on one of the kid's toys, which was causing the sharp pain in his back.

"Bubba, as far as I can tell, you're fine," Cathy gently explained.

"You're sure I'm not dying? My back does feel a lot better. That's kind of funny. Can I have a last beer?"

"I am going to go find Steele and the kids," Sandra stated and left the room shaking her head and rolling her eyes.

"Let's shackle his legs and keep him cuffed until tomorrow, and yes, you can have a beer," stated a relieved Bruce.

"Cool," said Bubba, he looked much better now that he was breathing slower.

"Can I have one too?" asked Cleo. Fran and Cleo plopped down beside the smiling Bubba.

"I guess you either got lucky, or zombie bites don't pass the virus," I stated.

"Let's keep an eye on him the rest of the day and night and see what tomorrow brings," Bruce replied. We took turns on both a watch outside the compound and inside the compound. Cleo and Fran never left Bubba's side that night.

Chapter 34: Parting

The next morning, we awoke to Cleo and Fran screaming. By the time we got to the lobby, the screaming had stopped. Bubba was sitting up, obviously confused and disheveled, but not a zombie. Fran and Cleo were laughing nervously and apologizing to Bubba for scaring him.

"What the heck is going on?" I asked, still in my boxers and light blue kitty shirt. Hey, it's comfortable.

"I woke up and saw Bubba covered in a blanket from head to toe, and I thought the worst," stated Cleo. "And I just screamed," he added.

Everyone else not on guard duty had made it to the lobby. Bubba was fine but groggy, as was everyone else. We uncuffed him, and we all went to the kitchen to eat. Sandra looked at my shirt and shook her head. Her head shakes a lot. We had a celebratory breakfast over Bubba not being sick. All three hunters confirmed Bubba had been bit by one of the hippie zombies, possibly Sleepy Bob. We discussed what we knew of zombie bites, which was nothing other than the fiction we were all exposed to. We speculated that the bite was not severe enough to spread the infection, or maybe he was just lucky. We also discussed how the zombie bug could be spread.

Bubba reported he felt fine, and it was time for them to head to his uncle Ronnie's cabin. His faithful companion Cleo agreed. Fran was just overjoyed having Bubba healthy and was fine with moving on.

We switched out Cleo's shotgun for another loaned AR-15 with ammo. We thought that Ronald might need the extra firepower with the additional mouths to feed. We also gave the trio a case of beer, which touched Bubba and Cleo's hearts deeply. We traded contact information and said our goodbyes.

Steele and I agreed to walk with them until we reached the road my house was on. The groups parted ways without incident. Steele and I tended to the animals and checked the perimeter of the house. We then went to Cathy's property and checked everything there. As we were walking back to my compound to get a beer and then head back, we saw smoke rising. It seemed to be coming from beyond the alligator farm. We skipped the beer and made our way back to the alligator farm carefully.

The others had seen the smoke and guessed it was between here and Dixon City. They attempted to call the McCormick's, who owned the barn that was close to the trail we used. There was no response to our calls.

Since Steele and I were already prepped for a hike and armed, it was agreed that we would bike out and see what was going on. We increased our AR-15 magazine totals to five each, and we both had a Glock 19 with three magazines each. The rest of the compound was on high alert.

We tried to be careful but also kept a brisk pace and got to the barn quicker than was safe. The barn was smoldering and had fire damage but was not burnt to the ground. There was a group of four people gathered to one side of the barn. One person was lying down, and two men and a lady were standing close by, and all were armed with hunting rifles, which were pointed in our direction.

We slowly got off our bikes and raised our hands, saying we saw the smoke and came to help. The younger McCormick recognized me, and they lowered their rifles. We approached and saw the older McCormick I had met lying on the ground.

They informed us that they caught a couple of bikers breaking into the barn. They had parked their motorcycles about a quarter mile down the road and walked through the fields to the barn. It was clear they knew the barn was there and it contained what they wanted. The two bikers made it to the barn before the McCormick's could challenge them. When the McCormick's yelled for them to come out with their hands up, the bikers set a corner of the barn on fire and came out shooting. They were shooting wildly, and the McCormick's let them run off rather than kill them. However, the senior McCormick had a little too much excitement and was out of his heart medication.

The senior McCormick was not dead but was obviously struggling. Steele and I kneeled down and spoke with him.

"How are you doing, old-timer?" I asked coolly.

Steele gave me a confused look but said nothing.

"I've been better, and why are you calling me old-timer? What is this, the 1890s? Aren't you the fella with the kitty shirt?" the older McCormick responded.

"We mostly ignore the dumb things that come out of his mouth, but he has his strengths," Steele stated, shaking his head and smiling. "What medication do you need?"

The McCormick's gave us the names of the two heart medications he needed. We discussed going to Dixon City or Crystal City, which was bigger. One of the McCormick clan wanted to go with Steele and me, but we suggested that they stay and guard the farm while we did our best to help out. We called in to the alligator farm, and through some discrete codes and communications, we informed our group we were headed to Dixion or beyond to help the farmers out. Cathy was less than happy but knows I am a tough guy and have hero-like tendencies. She lovingly calls it being a dummy.

The McCormick's gave us ten silver ounces to use in trade. They requested that if we could find an AR for sale, they would gladly pay up to thirty more silver ounces. We promised to see what we could find. We were all aware that the situation in Dixon and Crystal City could be very dangerous.

As we hopped back onto our bikes and prepared to head toward Dixon City, Steele looked over at me and said, "Old timer?"

"Hey, it sounded cool in my head."

Chapter 35: Shoot Out At The Fat Goat

It was getting dark, but we traveled until we reached the outskirts of Dixon City. We planned on camping outside of town and entering in the morning. We pushed our way into the woods and found a concealed space to camp for the night. We did not light a fire as we did not want to alert anyone to our presence.

The second hour into my watch, I heard a group coming down the path from Dixon City.

"Wait up, Zoey," a rough male voice said.

"We've got to keep moving," a young female voice replied.

An older voice called out, "What took you so long in town, Louis?"

"Man, I had to get all I can," Louis responded as they moved down the path and out of earshot.

The next morning, we hid our bikes and excess gear deep in the forest. Steele and I entered the town with our rifles, handguns, and ten silver ounce coins each. We saw foot traffic going in and out of the town on the roads, so there appeared to be some sort of order and freedom of movement.

When we entered the town, things appeared to be a mess. People were talking and bartering in the streets, and garbage was everywhere. There was a strong smell of sewage in the air, and most of the people reeked of body odor and were disheveled. Many of the people walking the streets were armed, and we detected no police presence. It was not at "Mad Max" level, but it was fast approaching.

We traveled to where the stores used to be and approached what used to be a pharmacy. The entrance was guarded by two armed men. Steele suggested I remain outside in case things went wrong. I suggested I go in and he waited, due to my advanced negotiation skills. Steele agreed I had good negotiation skills, but if a rescue was called for, "You're the man," Steele said. How could I argue with that?

I slyly stood staring across the street as Steele approached the entrance. He was stopped at the door and questioned. After some discussion, Steele displayed a few silver coins. The guards nodded their heads, then pointed at Steele's rifle. Steele shook his head "no," and they talked some more. One of the guards looked at me and seemed to relent in his discussion with Steele. They appeared to reach an agreement, but instead of going in, Steele wrote something on a piece of paper and gave it to one of the guards. He then turned and walked back to me.

"What happened?" I asked.

"They agreed to let me talk to the pharmacists but would not let me carry my guns inside. I told them I had silver to trade, but I was not going into the store unarmed. I mentioned I had backup across the street. After a little more discussion, they agreed to take a list to the pharmacist, and if he was interested, he would meet us at a pub called the Fat Goat within an hour with the medications."

We were interrupted by nearby gunfire. It sounded as if it were a block or less away. This did not seem to faze anyone on the crowded street. We both agreed to find the pub as soon as possible, meet the pharmacist, and then get the heck out of town as fast as we were able.

We stopped a random bum walking down the street for directions. The bum informed us he used to be the mayor of this town before the power died. He gave us detailed directions to the Fat Goat and requested two 9mm bullets for payment. The former mayor was so happy with the payment that he attempted to kiss me on the cheek. I stopped him and shook his hand.

"Why does everyone keep trying to kiss you?" asked Steele.

"I don't know, but I am taken. I should have worn my ring," I said as we made our way to the pub.

We followed the former mayor's directions. We heard the crowd before the establishment came into view. Business appeared to be brisk, to say the least. We approached the front door just as a couple of patrons were being thrown out for reasons unknown to us. We entered the pub and found a table that was likely just vacated. The table was close to a corner and allowed us both to sit with our backs to a wall and a view of the door. We sat down, and a waitress dressed in all leather and heavily armed demanded we order something or get out.

We both ordered a beer, at a cost of five 9mm shells each. The beer was a locally brewed batch of swill that we sipped slowly. A few minutes after our arrival, a man in an ill-fitting suit with a crew haircut and trimmed blond beard entered the pub carrying a small bag. He looked around, locked eyes on Steele, and approached our table.

"I'm Bub the pharmacist," was all he said, standing in front of us.

"Have a seat, partner," I replied smoothly.

Steele and Bub both stared at me for a moment before Bub took a seat. Bub smiled, showing his green and rotting teeth. I suspected he had a blue hoodie hanging in his closet at home. Pharmacist my foot.

"Gentlemen, you're in luck. The medications you are looking for are not in too much demand. I have a two year's supply of both medications, but it is going to cost you," Bub stated firmly, laying the package on the table and leaning back in his chair. As he leaned back, we got a glimpse of a revolver tucked in his pants.

We were about to respond when the former mayor stormed into the bar and yelled, "Where is he?"

Bub had his back to the man, but at the sound of the man's voice, his eyes got big. Bub jumped up and attempted to draw his gun. The former mayor was quite a bit faster and shot Bub twice in the chest as Steele and I watched with mouths open. Bub dropped to the ground as a couple of bouncers tackled the former mayor to the ground.

"Where the hell are we?" asked Steele to no one in particular, dazed.

"Was that the mayor?" I asked, in shocked confusion.

"Don't know, don't care. Let's grab the pills and get the hell out of this godforsaken place," Steele screamed over the commotion.

Steele discreetly picked up the package, and we walked around Bub's body. One of the bouncers holding the mayor to the ground informed us that we would need to give a statement to the town marshal. The other bouncer was wrestling the gun out of the former mayor's hands, asking where he got the gun and ammo.

We assured the bouncer we were heading there now. We got out the front door and started walking quickly towards the end of town.

"What the hell, are we in the Wild West?" I asked.

"Probably shouldn't have given the mayor those bullets," Steele said with his excellent hindsight.

"Oops," was all I could think of saying.

"Let's get the hell out of Dodge," Steele said.

"Dixon," I replied.

"Okay, partner," Steele stated, shaking his head and laughing.

"Hey, it sounded cool in my head," I replied as we picked up the pace out of town.

Chapter 36: Sundown

The sun was beginning to set as we reached the edge of town. We had gotten out of Dixon City without further incident. Soon after leaving town the road entered some woods. As we reached the area where we had to leave the road and head into the forest to retrieve our bikes, we heard the sound of motorcycles coming toward us. We dove into the forest and hid in the underbrush as the bikers rode by. After they passed, we got up and continued to where we stashed our bikes.

We approached our hiding spot quietly. We heard noises as we drew near. Steele and I were able to sneak up to the spot and viewed four zombies meandering around our bikes. We drew back slightly and discussed our options. We decided we could take them out without using guns. We did not want to attract the attention of the bikers or anyone else. We hid our rifles and kept our handguns on us just in case. We both found large sticks to use on the interlopers.

Steele and I snuck back to the hiding spot. I told Steele I would take out the biggest one first and then go from there. He smiled and agreed. We charged into the zombies and squared off.

I hit the largest zombie across his back hard. He stumbled forward and fell to the ground. He recovered quickly and charged at me clumsily. I darted to the side, but he grabbed my jacket as the big zombie fell to the ground, dragging me with him. He recovered quicker than I did and was on top of me as I grabbed his neck. His hands were on my shoulders, and he was attempting to lean down and bite my face. I tried to roll to the side, but the big zombie weighed too much for me to flip him off. I squeezed his neck as hard as I could, and his grip on my shoulders lessened, and he stopped trying to bite me. He let go of my shoulders, and I used the slight break to headbutt him in the nose.

The zombie rolled off me, and I struggled to my feet. I searched for my log and soon found it. I bent down and grabbed it just as the big zombie regained his footing. He lunged at me as I jumped to the side. I reared back and struck him with the log across the back of his head, and he dropped to the ground.

Breathing heavily and feeling as if the log weighed a ton, I spun around to face the next zombie. I discovered Steele sitting on the ground, smoking a cigarette, watching me. Around him lay three incapacitated zombies. Where did he get the cigarette?

"Good job, Jack," he complimented me as he got up with a slight pep in his step. "Time to go."

"Hang on, I need a minute. My zombie was a tough one," I informed Steele.

"Yes, I watched the whole thing," he informed me.

His zombies must have been in a further state of decay or were just weaker humans before they turned. Mine was obviously larger and much more ferocious. I brushed off the debris stuck to my clothing from rolling around on the ground, noticing that Steele didn't have a speck of dust on him. Ten minutes later I was ready to leave. We got on our bikes and made our way to the trail that led to the McCormick farm.

"Hey, you don't smoke," I declared.

"It's bad for you," Steele responded.

Chapter 37: Homeward Again

We biked quietly on the trails in the direction of the McCormick farm. A few miles from where we fought the zombies, we came across a patch on the trail where an obvious battle had taken place. The brush was smashed down, and there were bullet casings and blood on the ground. We stashed our bikes and searched the area. A few yards off the path we found the body of a young Hispanic male with his AR still in hand. He had no ID on him and was dressed like he belonged in a motorcycle gang. We took the AR and ammo and left the young fellow to the elements.

We traveled a few more miles and halted when we heard a voice telling us to stop. As soon as we heard the voice, we both jumped off our bikes and dove into the woods. We ended up on opposite sides of the trail, but we could still see each other.

"We don't want any more trouble, but we're armed and will shoot," stated a gruff sounding older man's voice.

"We are just passing through and don't want any trouble either," yelled Steele.

"How about we send one person out and you send one person out and we talk?" said the gruff voice.

"Fine with us," Steele replied.

"Frank, go talk to them," said the gruff voice.

"Why do I have to go, William? Send Louis," replied a younger voice.

"Oh hell, I'll go," stated a female voice.

Steele pointed at me and then the path. I guess I was going to meet the female while Steele covered me. I got up with my AR in the low-ready position and walked a little way up the path, within eyesight of Steele. A moment later a young white lady in a red sweatshirt approached me with a handgun in her hand at the low ready also.

"Hi, I'm Zoey," she informed me.

"I'm Jack, and my buddy covering us is Steele," I said.

"Louis, Frank, and William are behind me. What are you doing out here? Sorry we are being cautious; we were ambushed last night by a couple of biker guys," she informed me.

"We saw the remains, looks like you got one of them. We found his body in the woods."

"Good, I hope his friend got shot too. William, I think we are good, no way is this guy in a gang," Zoey said.

I guess I was just too polished and well-spoken to be confused with a hooligan. "Steele, I think we are good here. They appear friendly enough."

Zoey's friends all came out armed but nonaggressive. Louis was a young black man dressed in a shirt and tie, Frank was a young white man with a goatee and the look of a weightlifter. William looked like an older version of Bruce and was dressed in military clothes. We all shook hands and sat down in the clearing the group was occupying when we stumbled upon them.

The group informed us they had left Crystal City a few days ago as things began to deteriorate, and food became harder to find. They made it to Dixon City, but felt it was worse than Crystal City. They were moving south, looking for a small town or farm to wait this event out. They were camping last night when two thugs stumbled into their camp. Both groups were surprised, but the bikers pulled out their guns, assuming they were easy targets. They were mistaken, and after an exchange of gunfire, Zoey's group thought the thugs had run off. They did not know that one had died. They all agreed he deserved what he got, and the world would not miss him much.

Steele and I told the group we knew of a farm that might need some extra hands if they were willing to work and defend the property. Steele told them there was no guarantee they would take them on and that they may not need the help. If they did not need help, we would aid them on their way south. They reported that it sounded good, and we agreed to continue on together.

We made it to the McCormick farm a few hours later. As we approached the barn, a voice called out, ordering us to stop where we were and state our business. We yelled out to the unseen guards, and one of the McCormick's came out of hiding to speak with us. After assuring the guard that the newcomers were not a threat, we were allowed onto the property, and the younger McCormick was summoned.

We made introductions and made our suggestions about having the group help out at the farm. The younger McCormick reported that they could use some help, but that was up to his father. He informed us that his father had been bedbound since we left, and his condition was unchanged. We gave the young McCormick the package of medication, their ten silver coins, and the AR-15 and ammo we took from the dead biker.

The young McCormick and the guard were shocked at our generosity and urged us to take the silver coins at least. We refused and just said if we ever needed help, just return the favor. We told them we needed to get home to the compound. The younger McCormick agreed to house the new group and have them talk to his father when he recovered. He warned us that the bikers had made another attempt to raid their supplies but were scared off before gunfire erupted. We made our goodbyes and were on our way. We arrived at the alligator farm without further incident.

Chapter 38: Friend From Afar

We woke the next morning to a group of men loitering in our parking lot. How they got so close without us detecting them was a mystery. Spirit called us when she saw them, and I ran to the gate as quickly as I could. I climbed up the catwalk and looked out on the group of visitors. There were eight men, casually dressed in jeans and t-shirts. They were all light complected and had beards and mustaches. They were armed with rifles and all of them had handguns and hatchets on their belts. All the weapons were on their shoulders or holsters, and they made no aggressive moves. They also did not attempt to communicate with us.

"Ummm, can I help you?" I asked loudly.

They all looked my way smiling, still making no sound. One of the group, a man in his early forties, with long blond hair and an athletic build stepped forward and said, "No, but we thank you for asking." He then turned back to the group and spoke quietly.

"Riggs to Wiener, sitrep," radioed Bruce.

"I don't know who they are, what they want, or why they are here, but I like them. Let me see if I can get some more information," I responded.

"Hey, do you guys need some help or anything?" I asked.

The same man responded again with a polite smile, "No, we are good. Thank you," and turned around to speak quietly with his group.

"These guys are cool," stated Spirit.

"I bet they have cool names too," I commented.

"Why are you hanging out in front of our compound?" I asked.

"Forgive us, we can leave if you wish," the polite man responded.

"No, you're good. Sure we can't get you anything? Maybe some cold water?"

"Cold water would be nice. Thank you," the tall man with long hair responded with a smile.

"Wheeler to Riggs, can you bring a couple of pitchers of cold water and glasses to the gate?"

"What the hell is going on? Who are they and what do they want?" Bruce demanded.

"I still don't know who they are, what they want, or what's going on, but I offered them cold water and they accepted." I relayed to Bruce.

"I am coming down there now," Bruce stated.

"Don't forget the water and cups," Spirit chimed in.

"Dammit, I won't forget," Bruce snapped.

The group seemed to finish their discussion, and all sat down about 10 feet from our front gate and faced us, most with pleasant smiles on their face. A few minutes later Bruce and Cathy appeared with pitchers and cups. Bruce instructed me and Spirit to cover them so they could open the gate and give them water. Spirit and I hesitantly unshouldered our rifles and kept them at the low ready. Bruce opened the gate slowly and walked out with the pitchers and glasses. The group politely took the glass given to them and when their glasses were filled, they thanked Cathy and Bruce and drank the water.

"How do you get the water so cold?" asked the presumed leader.

"We have limited electricity and have a freezer running," Bruce minimized our situation without lying.

"You are the first people to offer assistance to us since the power went out. We don't need any assistance, but it is nice to see there are still those that care for others. We have heard that you have helped a few others recently. We came to see who you were. We come from the land of ice and snow."

"Oh, you're Inuit's," I responded.

"Um, no we aren't Inuit's, but that's irrelevant," the leader clarified.

"Would you like to come in and rest? It is safe here," Bruce offered.

"We are safe wherever we go, but we thank you for the offer. Since we feel you are good people, we have news for you. We have seen men with leather vests walking the woods around your compound. They are watching you. They ride motorcycles and hide them down the highway and walk up and watch you," said the leader of the group.

"So, you have been watching us too?" I asked.

"No, we were watching the watchers," he answered.

"When they aren't here who are you watching?" I asked.

"Uh, no one," he answered.

"I am closing our drapes from now on," I said.

"Your bed is heart shaped," he quietly stated.

"What?" I asked.

"Nothing," replied the long-haired man from the land of the ice and snow who was not an Inuit.

"Thank you for the warning, we will be more vigilant. Are you sure there is nothing we can give you?" asked Bruce.

"We are fine and wish you well," was his parting words. The group all got up and walked into the woods, leaving no trace.

"Who the hell were those guys?" asked Bruce.

"I don't know but they sure were cool," was Cathy's summation.

"I bet they had cool names too," I commented again.

Chapter 39: Leather And Chains

The next day had started out calm enough. It was over three weeks since the EMP hit and zombies and rioters took over. Spirit was at the front gate around noon when she called in that she heard vehicles approaching. Bruce manned the tower with Sandra and a couple of sniper rifles. Cathy, Steele, and I joined Spirit at the front gate with our rifles. Colby and Brie were on guard duty in the visitor center lobby and kept an eye on the rear of the alligator farm.

I joined Spirit at the top of the front gate, while Cathy manned the catwalk one section to the right and Steele one section to the left of the front gate. It only took a few minutes for us to get into positions with rifles pointing toward the driveway and us as low as possible to give as small a target as possible. I switched my radio off and told everyone to turn their radios down.

A line of fifteen motorcycles appeared on the driveway and spread out when they reached the parking area. Most of the motorcycles had solitary riders, but there were two or three with two passengers. They were all wearing black leather vests, but since they were all facing us, we could not see if they had patches on the back.

Three bikers approached the front gate and stopped about forty feet from it. The group of fifteen bikers cut their engines at the same time, which was annoyingly cool. The lead center rider had a black balaclava covering his face, to keep the dust off his face or to look scary. He got off his bike and stepped forward.

I said, "That's far enough. Who are you and what do you want?"

"We are looking for a place to rest and recharge," responded the front man with a slight Spanish accent.

"Well, no offense, but keep looking."

As soon as I finished the word "looking," the remaining 14-plus bikers all hopped off their bikes and had guns pointed in our direction in one smooth motion. I bet they all had tough guy names too.

"We don't want to hurt you, we just want the alligator farm. We are the Iron

Conquistadors, and we take what we want," he said in an all-too-familiar voice.

"Rico, don't make me shoot you," I said to one of the former residents of Cell Block B in the prison where I worked. I realized this was likely the same Rico that was involved in the recent drug activity.

"Officer Emily?" Rico asked, his tough-guy voice discarded.

The Iron Conquistadors were a local motorcycle "club" that was a one-percenter group. When the word club is used to describe a motorcycle group, it usually means they are a gang. One percenter means they are criminals. The Iron Conquistadors were affiliated with a larger "club," and they had more than 15 members locally unless things changed drastically.

Rico spent two years in B Block for breaking into a rival "club's" hangout and vandalizing it. He also drank as much of their alcohol as he could and passed out in the parking lot. Luckily, he was found by the police before the rival club members showed up. Rico did not cause problems while in the prison and even helped keep the peace between rival factions in the jail from time to time. He was respectful to the guards and was obviously intelligent when compared to the average biker.

I also now suspected he was dealing methamphetamine with a couple of fools in Dixon City.

"Where is the rest of your crew?" I asked, not expecting an honest answer.

"Oh, they're around," was Rico's response.

That was a bad sign, he probably had people in the woods with rifles pointed at us. "We have about twenty people in our little community, so I think it would be best if you moved on," I threatened Rico halfheartedly.

"No, with the two that arrived a week ago, you have seven adults and two kids." They must not have seen Father Roger leave, but it was apparent they had been watching us. "I like you Officer Emily, so I am going to give you time to pack up and leave. Take what you want on your bikes and leave. We will be back in two days. If you are still here, we will feed you to the alligators. Oh, and don't start shooting. You know we have more than these guns you see pointed at you. We would take this place now, but I want to show you some courtesy since you showed me some. I would also like to avoid losing some of my club members. You have two more nights. We will be here at noon two days from now."

Rico and his entourage got on their bikes, turned around, and rode off in a cloud of dust and noise. The noise seemed to attract the hippies because soon after the bikers left, we saw the zombies shuffling out of the woods. We kept low so the hippies would not see us and leave. We did not see Father Roger. We figured he was trying to catch up with them, or they ate him.

Chapter 40: More Time

Seeing the zombies gather after the bikers left gave us some food for thought. We weren't sure what we were going to do, but we had a plan that would, at the very least, give us more time, and if we were lucky, improve our chances of effectively dealing with the biker gang.

While I was debating with Rico, Bruce was watching through his sniper rifle scope. He and Sandra had the bright idea of sending up a drone Bruce had so we could track them to where they were staying. Had they not had this timely idea, we would have had to have tried tracking them.

Bruce had some high-quality equipment, including some long-range, small drones with cameras. They sent the drone as high up as quickly and discreetly as they could. They hoped to evade the detection of the bikers that were likely spying on us from the woods. Sandra and Bruce tracked them to a campground about four miles away. They seemed to have taken over a primitive campground with about ten one-room cabins. These cabins appeared to have had no electricity even before the electricity went down.

This was likely the source of the smoky campfire we saw a few days ago.

We left Cathy in the guard tower to keep watch, and the rest of us met to discuss our options. "Noise seems to attract the zombies. So, we need a way to attract the zombies to the biker's campsite," Sandra stated.

"I have just what we need to accomplish that, but someone is going to have to sneak in pretty close to do it," Bruce said.

I had been preparing for this my entire adult life, well, at least the last five years. I was a faithful acolyte of the teachings of Jeff Cooper. I mastered the art of the seven principles of personal protection. I had honed my skills of stealth and combat to become an implement of death. I was the obvious choice to go. Boy, would Cathy worry.

"Steele should go," Bruce and Sandra said at the same time. I was probably too valuable to be risked on such an excursion.

"I have boxes full of fireworks. Steele can sneak out at night and set up a delayed series of fireworks that will hopefully attract the zombies to the bikers and let them fight it out. That would slow down Rico's plans and maybe reduce their numbers," Bruce schemed.

When night fell, we used Bruce's infrared goggles and spotted two watchers in the woods, quite some distance from our fortress. Infrared or night vision goggles picked up heat signatures such as body heat and worked well in darkness. They were camped alone, one on each side of the driveway, quite some distance apart.

Steele struck out with two duffle bags full of fireworks and fuses. The plan was to string up a long-lasting fireworks display with enough of a delay for Steele to sneak off into the woods surrounding the campsite. He was careful not to be seen by the two spies and trotted off to his destination.

We gave Steele the call sign "Williams," and Sandra was given the call sign "Ash". Damn it, I could have been "Iron Man". Sorry, I had just thought of that.

Around 1:00 am Steele called in, "Williams to Ash, the stage is set, the band plays in ten minutes. Going to miss the show. Keep the home fire burning."

I turned to Cathy to interpret for her, but she stated, "I know what he meant, you dummy." She said with a wink and a gentle smile. How the heck did she know I was going to pass that information on? I picked a winner.

Ten minutes after Steele signed off, we heard distant booms. "I'll get the drone up about ten minutes after the show ends and see if we attracted the attention we hoped for. Steele should be back in a little over an hour if he moves fast," Bruce stated.

Chapter 41: Party Of Three

The drone was sent heading towards the biker camp after things quieted down. We crowded around Bruce's small laptop to view what the drone could pick up. After a few minutes he found the biker camp. The camp was a cluster of small cabins set in a clearing in a circle with one driveway leading into it. The entire area was surrounded by thick forest.

The bikers were obviously on edge and high alert. They had bonfires burning between most of the cabins. The bikers were all armed and facing out from the center of camp. They looked very anxious, and there was plenty of evidence of earlier heavy drinking. The bikers were talking loudly and scanning the woods for the source of the fireworks.

The gang members appeared to quiet down, and some turned to the east as if they heard something coming through the woods. "This should be the zombies, I hope they are spread out and do some damage to these dirt bags," Bruce stated eloquently. The rest of us gently jockeyed for position to watch the drama unfold. The kids were in the tower keeping watch with the night vision goggles. We continued to try to spare them as much horror as possible in this new harsh world.

"Oh crap," Bruce exclaimed.

"What? Why oh crap?" Sandra asked.

"Those aren't the zombies, the religious nuts walked into the camp, and the bikers are shooting. Looks like the church guys were confused at first, and some are running away; some were close enough to use their staffs."

"Oops," both Cathy and I said.

"Didn't think of that possibility," I observed.

"Oh crap."

"What? Why oh crap again?" Sandra shrieked.

"The zombie hippies just entered from the north of camp. Looks like complete chaos. I think some of the bikers are panic shooting and hitting some of their own. Looks like Rico is trying to take control of his group."

"Oh crap," again, observed Bruce.

"What?" screamed Sandra, who is usually quite subdued and in control.

"Looks like Rico took a shot to the arm. He is up and looks pissed though. Seems like most of the religious nuts ran off. Strange, looks like a lot of the zombies also left. There are quite a few bodies lying around. At least four of them look like bikers, and a few more of the bikers look like they took a good beating."

We had hoped the zombies would have done more. We felt a little guilty about the Pathetic Souls stumbling in on the camp. People should be more careful and less trusting during a zombie apocalypse for goodness sake. They learned a valuable lesson that day, well, the ones that lived anyway. Oops.

At least we got the bikers' numbers down a few. They were beaten up a bit and they probably won't be well rested for the next couple of days. It is not every day a bunch of dudes in robes and a bunch of hippie zombies stumble into your camp. That must take a toll, even for tough-guy bikers.

When Steele returned, we gathered around the dinner table and discussed our options. We discussed leaving. We discussed defensive tactics. We discussed what to do with the kids if we decided to stay and fight.

Chapter 42: Pack Or Play

We decided we were going to stay and fight. We had the defensive position. We were familiar with the terrain and had night vision goggles, so we ruled the dark. We had the higher ground. The Iron Conquistadors could only attack from two points, the driveway on bikes or the back trail on foot, the rest was swamp. We also knew from experience that if we kept our heads down and made a lot of noise, we would have the remaining zombie visitors to help us. Heck, maybe the Pathetic Souls would want some payback. Probably not.

We also had a few fully automatic weapons, which require a special permit that Bruce obtained years ago. We needed to get the kids out of the area though. So, I hopped on my bike and had the kids follow me to our home. From there we checked the house and fed the animals. I had the kids get their small hunting rifles that were usually locked up. County folk often teach their kids how to hunt at a young age, they also tend to pound in the rules of gun safety.

We then biked to Gilbert and Jane Fountain's home and called out loudly before getting close to the house. There was no answer.

We approached the front door and knocked, yelling that it was "Jack Emily". They were not home, so I left a note telling them we had problems with a biker gang and I was leaving the kids at home armed. I requested they check in on the kids and, if able, keep them until we returned to retrieve them. I wrote that the gang would be attacking us at noon tomorrow. I left one of my radios on their doorstep and wrote down the channel they could use to reach the kids. I stuck the note on the door with a piece of gum. Man, does gum come in handy. I put another piece of gum in my mouth and left the Fountains' property.

I brought the kids back to our house. Brie and Colby both begged to come back with me. I am not sure how seriously I was taking the apocalypse until that moment. There was a good chance I would not be around to see them grow up. Should we surrender our prime location and fall back to our home? Tough guy talk aside, do we allow thugs and criminals to take what they want? If we started running now, we would be running for the rest of our lives. We would make a stand. Gilbert and Jane Fountain were friends and would care for the kids if needed. I kissed my crying children and told them I would be back in two days and to stay here and look for the Fountains. The kids knew it was a bad situation, but I don't think they were old enough to realize just how dire the coming events were.

On the way back, I set up tripwires on the path to our house. Tripwires are thin, hard-to-see wires strung across a path that are triggered when stepped through. What they trigger depends on what you want. My trip wires were set to fire off shotgun shells directed at the ground. The purpose of these was not to harm people (or wandering animals) but to make a noise loud enough for the kids to hear.

I wanted to keep as many animals away from the tripwires as possible. I read that animals are scared off by human urine, so I began to urinate around the path. While in the middle of marking my territory, out popped old Robert. Awkward moment. We made direct eye contact with each other, and both of us froze. Since my hands were occupied, I did the only thing I could think of doing. I spit my gum at his face. The gum sailed through the air and bounced harmlessly off his forehead.

Robert started to groan and advance towards me. I stumbled backwards and fumbled while trying to be decent again. I kept stumbling back and set off one of the tripwires. The loud bang startled the heck out of me, and I didn't startle easy! You try backpedaling while trying to become decent while also being chased by a well-dressed zombie with two big, shoeprints on his chest. Interestingly, the loud bang seemed to startle the zombie somewhat too. Robert stopped and looked for the cause of the noise, giving me the time I needed to become presentable again. There were still three more tripwires set, so no need to reset the triggered one. The electric fence seemed to keep Robert away from the house. Old Robert was between me and my bike and rifle. I didn't really want to shoot my zombie neighbor unless I had too anyway. Robert snapped out of his daze and began coming at me. For the third time that I know of, Robert got a heavy boot to the chest, sending him flying into the woods again. I got on my bike and took off, making as much noise as I could in the hope that Robert would follow me.

I made it back to the compound before dark and set some tripwires close to the back trail entrance. We met in the watchtower so we could keep watch and make plans. I made sure Bruce had washed his hands and then ate the dinner he made. Past dysentery aside, Bruce was a good cook.

Bruce passed out night vision goggles and bulletproof vests to us all. "What the hell, Bruce? You had vests all this time and are just now passing them out?" I asked in my friendly manner.

"I didn't think the hippies, or the congregation, were going to shoot at us, so I did not bother with them." He had a good point.

We spent the rest of the day fortifying the walls and gate. We put a couple strands of barbed wire along the top of the entire wall. We placed extra ammo hidden along the walls and on the catwalks. Cathy, Spirit, and Steele had AR-15s. Sandra and I had M4A's, which could be fired fully automatic if selected. Bruce had a Remington 700 set up for long-range sniper shots.

We scattered nails all over the driveway and the parking lot. The bikers would have to walk their way down the driveway, giving us plenty of time to defend ourselves and giving them plenty of time to rethink their choices in life.

This is a good time to discuss a gunfight. There are a lot of versions of the rules to a gun fight. I will simplify them for simplicity's sake.

Do everything you can to avoid a gunfight. Give up your wallet, give up your car keys if you're not in your car, walk or run away from the situation if you can leave safely and not abandon others to harm.

If you draw or raise your weapon, you must fear that you or others will suffer grave bodily injury, and you have no way to stop or avoid the situation peacefully.

After you raise your weapon, unless the adversary turns tail and runs, you pull the trigger and aim for center mass. Center mass is the chest. Not the legs and not the head. If you are at this point, the adversary has made their choice, and the time for mercy is past. Legs may not stop an aggressor, and with your adrenaline pumping, it is easy to miss a head, even at close range. Also take notice if the aggressor runs, as he may be running to get a weapon or for cover and to fire from a safer position.

The next and last rule is, once you are at the point of pulling the trigger, win at all costs.

Only a fool will fight fairly. In a gunfight, your responsibility is to win by all means necessary. Stop shooting when your aggressor is no longer a threat to anyone. If possible, keep moving. A moving target is much harder to hit.

Also remember to watch what is behind or in front of your target. I did not bring up the rules of a gunfight earlier because I did not mean to shoot Pantless Poncho Zombie Guy. True, he was a zombie, but he was an unarmed zombie.

The gun nuts say if you are not shooting, you should be reloading; if you are not shooting or reloading, your adversary is dead, or you're dead. Keep in mind most gun nuts have never been in a gunfight.

Chapter 43: Late Night Excursion

We met before bedtime and discussed what to do about the two bikers that were spying on us. We were all constantly reminded of their presence due to their constant urge to smoke cigarettes and stronger substances which blew into our compound. They were not discreet and sure weren't slick.

"I think we should sneak up on them and take them out," stated Bruce.

"You mean kill them?" Spirit asked, shocked.

"We don't have to kill them; we could shoot them with tranquilizer darts and tie them up."

"Why do you have tranquilizer guns?" I asked suspiciously.

"This is an alligator farm, every now and then I need to subdue a gator, dummy."

"Someone would have to get awfully close to shoot them with a tranquilizer gun," Sandra observed.

This was my moment to shine. My years of preparation would finally come to fruition. I was a finely tuned machine ready to be unleashed. I could move silently and was invisible in the shadows. I was invincible, but not like eccentric Willy.

"Steele should go," both Bruce and Sandra stated at the same time. I was honored at how protective they were of me.

Steele got into all dark clothing and was briefed on the use of the dart gun. Bruce assured Steele the darts were more than powerful enough to knock out the targets, and the darts would kick in under a minute. That meant that he had to shoot his target and not get shot for about a minute. It also meant that if the first biker did shoot, it would warn the other watcher to be on high alert. If they had radio communication, it could get ugly if the remaining watcher called his fellow spy.

Steele once again trotted off into the woods. Not as stealthy as I would have, but pretty darn quietly. The watchers were quite spread out, and we hoped they did not have night vision.

A couple of hours later Steele called in, reporting he had darted and tied up both bikers and needed help bringing them to the compound. Sondra, Bruce, and I went to help Steele bring back the bikers while Spirit and Cathy stood watch.

If you have never tried to carry an unconscious adult male wearing biker leather, I recommend passing on the opportunity. It took an hour each to lug them back to the compound. Bruce brought the handcuffs and shackles. I have no idea why he had so many, but at least they were not the fuzzy ones.

We put them in a metal-walled closet in the storage area of the first floor. They were handcuffed to chairs. Good thing there was an apocalypse, or we would have all kinds of legal charges, including kidnapping. One of the guys looked similar to Rico. Both appeared to be in good health and were still out cold. We searched them and took everything but their undershirts and boxers.

With the zombie raid and darting the spies, we had reduced their numbers by at least six. They both carried radios and started receiving calls around 2:00 am. We figured out

"IC" stood for Iron Conquistadors, and "Watcher One" and "Watcher Two" were the call signs for the spying bikers. How unoriginal and lacking in imagination. Rico's voice sounded very upset when he did not get a response, especially from "Watcher One".

Chapter 44: Talk Time

The morning of our deadline came with a bright sunrise that had little to no breeze. We touched bases with Crazy Tom and Paranoid Billy. They both said the other preppers they spoke with were reporting no change in the situation and most were still successfully isolated. They wished us luck, and we assured them we would check in after the battle.

We sat down to a healthy meal, knowing it may well be our last, or that some of us may not be there for our next meal. We had discussed all of us dressing in camo, because that seemed like the thing to do. Cathy and Sandra pointed out that there was no use for that and suggested we all wear whatever we wanted.

At the breakfast table sat Cathy, dressed in her "hippy" jeans and a black shirt. Spirit was in her now-cleaned sundress and combat boots. Bruce wore his camos, but he always wore camos. Steele wore a black shirt, black pants, and a black balaclava, which would look stupid if he weren't so darn cool. Sandra wore an expensive sweat suit and tennis shoes. I decided to wear my cowboy hat, western vest, Colby's toy sheriff badge, cowboy boots, and a big fake mustache.

Sandra came to the table last and sat down. She scanned the table and froze when she saw me. She then spoke one word, "Weiner." What the hell did she know? This was followed by a bunch of snort laughs.

We began eating what could be the last meal for all or some of us. Little was said at first, but we livened up after we started eating. If we died today, we wanted to have some joy before it happened. Cathy and I worried we had made a poor choice and should have been cowering at home with the kids.

After breakfast we said a short prayer. We then checked our weapons. All of us had a rifle and a handgun. We then put on our bulletproof vests, which really screwed up Spirit's outfit, but she did not seem to mind. I gave everyone a stick of gum. I chugged a Yoo-hoo, and we went to our assigned spots.

Bruce was stationed in the watchtower as overwatch. Overwatch means he was providing cover for the rest of us. I was at the front gate with Sandra. Cathy was two wall sections over to the right, and Steele was two sections over to the left. Spirit was at the top of the back gate, armed and ready. We all had our radios handy, and I had reminded everyone my call sign was "Wheeler."

Bruce sent the drone up around 11:45 am to see what could be seen. Man, do I hate punctual bikers. Bruce informed us on the radio that they were on their way. Bruce had a surprise for all of us. A few minutes after he notified us of the imminent arrival of Iron Conquistadors, he started firing off fireworks again. Hey, it worked once!

Soon we heard the distant roar of the bikes approaching. I had my handy binoculars out and scanned the driveway leading to the parking lot. I was really anxious, and the Yoo-hoos were not sitting well in my stomach. "Is that your stomach?" asked Sandra.

"I don't feel so good," was my response.

"You look like an idiot dressed like that, and you better not throw up. You should have known better than to chug chocolate milk and then run out into the sun." Sandra got on the radio, breaking radio silence, "I want a new spot.

Wiener is going to puke on me." I heard Cathy and Steele both laugh. Must be nerves.

Bruce responded, "Riggs to Ash, maintain radio silence. You're stuck with Weiner." This drew more nervous laughter from Cathy and Steele.

Radio silence was maintained for about 30 seconds before a loud report came from the back of the compound. Spirit reported, "The hippies are here and heading for the parking lot. They look pretty ragged, and the swamp is slowing them down."

The bikers stopped soon after turning into the driveway. After the first four or five bike tires blew, the others pulled to the side of the driveway and started walking down the long driveway, with fireworks still going off above them.

Halfway down the driveway they stopped. We were scanning them with our binoculars to see what shady plan they were implementing. It seemed like they were just tired and were taking a break. It was hot out, and it was a long driveway. After a five-minute break, just three bikers continued the trip toward the gate. It was the same three that came forward at the last meeting.

"I probably shouldn't have eaten those smoked oysters," I said over my increasingly loud stomach.

"You idiot. Chocolate milk and oysters on a hot day, with a shootout scheduled?" Sandra helpfully stated.

"Yoo-hoo is not chocolate milk! It is nectar of the gods!" I clarified while my stomach continued to grumble ever louder.

Rico and his partners made it to our front gate, obviously tired and sweaty. Rico's arm was in a sling and was bandaged. "How the hell did you talk a bunch of hippies and monks into attacking us? That was nuts. Hell, it was downright terrifying!"

"We have many allies," I replied, followed by a loud, unexpected belch that caused Sandra to step to the side and the three visitors to take a step back. I thought it was a good response, but the stupid belch stole its thunder.

"I don't know why you are still here, and if you did anything to my brother, I will make you pay," he said those last five words very slowly and quite loudly too. That explained the resemblance of Watcher One. My stomach began to protest loudly again.

"If you ever want to see him again, you will turn around and leave now." I coughed, and my stomach again grumbled loudly. Sweat broke out on my brow. I began taking deep breaths.

"Are you okay, Officer Emily?" Rico asked with genuine confusion and maybe a dash of concern.

"I am fine." The word "fine" must have been a trigger for my stomach. This was not my proudest moment. I began projectile vomiting Yoo-hoo and oysters down on our visitors. When I stopped, all three were covered in vomit, completely still, and utterly shocked.

Without another word, the three emissaries turned and stomped off. Their anger was as pronounced as the stench of Yoo-hoo and oysters.

"Holy hell," Sandra stated, bewildered. "You're an idiot."

"Sitrep. What's going on?", asked Spirit.

"Looks like Weiner just threw up on Rico and two of his buddies. Pretty sure the peace talks are over," Bruce informed Spirit.

Sandra had a few moments to process what had occurred and added, "What is wrong with you?"

Like I said, it was not my proudest moment, but pretty darn funny. Besides, I felt a lot better now. I got a piece of gum to help my breath.

Chapter 45: Battle Time

The angry bikers walked back to the group. Spreading nails out appeared to be a good idea. The three bikers looked exhausted when they rejoined the group. The rest of the group shied away from them, probably because they were covered in vomit. The three sat down in the shade and tried to clean up as best they could.

After a five-minute break, the group of about twenty bikers started walking their way to the compound with rifles in hand. It was a very hot day, and the bikers were all wearing their leather vests and chaps. When they came within rifle range, Bruce fired a warning shot. Apparently, Burce is a hell of a shot, or darn lucky. His shot hit one of the lead hooligan's rifles, scaring the hell out of the rifle carrier and those around him. It also rendered the gun useless.

The bikers stopped and spread out, going into the woods on both sides of the driveway. The forest came close to the walls of the compound, which provided cover for the bikers as they approached.

We could hear them approaching in the woods. Bruce stated, "Don't worry about kill shots, wounded enemies draw their friends in to help them, which reduces their numbers. These aren't hardened soldiers, the screaming will freak them out too. Shoot at will."

We all had our heads slightly above the walls with our rifles scanning the area. I caught sight of a biker creeping through the woods toward us. I lined up my shot, aiming for center mass, exhaled, and fired, striking him in the leg.

He screamed at the top of his lungs and dropped to the ground. Two of his buddies ran to him, pulling him behind a large tree. A shot from the woods hit the wall close to my head, and I dropped. Both groups started firing, and chaos ensued. Both sides were screaming, and pieces of wood, dust, and gun smoke filled the air. We had the slight advantage due to our elevated position and better cover, though the sheet metal would not stop a rifle shot.

There was a lot of gunfire and yelling from the woods, so more than one was probably hit. I looked around just as Steele took a round to his chest and arm. The chest shot was blocked by the bulletproof vest, but the arm shot was bleeding, and the chest shot knocked the wind out of him. We were all pinned down with their superior numbers firing at us.

The bikers were getting closer to the clearing between the wall and the forest. One of us would pop up every now and then and get a shot off. We were getting desperate, but thankfully the zombie hippies arrived. In the heat of battle and with all the screaming, the zombies were forgotten by the bikers, and at least a few were involved in hand-to-hand combat with the ten or more zombies.

This distraction gave us the opportunity to get some more well-placed shots at the bikers, incapacitating more of them. Ten minutes after the zombies arrived, they were either shot or had run off. The bikers appeared to retreat, to regroup, we assumed.

During the pause in the fighting, Cathy ran to Steele and helped him bandage the wounded arm. His chest hurt, and the bullet wound to his arm went completely through but missed any bones. Bruce radioed in, reporting that the bikers had regrouped back down the driveway. Bruce said he could count at least twelve of them standing and five or six on the ground wounded or possibly dead.

The bikers were all gathered around and likely planning something. We reloaded our magazines and prepared for a second attack. We were winded from the attack and used this time to rest, drink, and snack.

We received a radio call from the McCormick's. They had heard the gunfire, and the younger McCormick and Frank came to investigate. They told us they would make their way to the back of the compound and help. Spirit was warned of their coming and told not to shoot. We appreciated the much-needed help. The bikers did not appear to be monitoring the radio.

Chapter 46: Second Wave

With McCormick and Frank up front, our defenses improved significantly. McCormick brought a nice hunting rifle with a scope. Though the bikers had gathered about a half mile from us, the young McCormick said he could reduce their numbers a little more. He did not want to kill anyone unless he had to though. He took aim at the distant bikers, and after a few seconds, squeezed his trigger. One of the bikers dropped, and new screams could be heard. McCormick had shot the man in the foot.

The bikers scattered to both sides of the woods along the driveway. Frank suggested shooting at their bikes parked at the end of the driveway if he thought he could hit them. Up for the challenge, the young McCormick started taking shots at the bikes. This caused the bikers to scramble yet again and move their bikes even farther back. They were getting plenty of exercise at this point and quite the worse for wear.

We saw them break up into two groups and begin their approach again through the woods on both sides of the driveway. They had a long walk, so we got comfortable. The zombies would not be there to help this time, but we now had Frank and the young McCormick, and they were down at least five bikers.

When they got close, we started taking shots at them and tried to pin them down or hit them if possible. The shooting got heated, and Frank had his ear nicked by a bullet, but other than some blood and discomfort, he was fine.

Bruce radioed in that he had spotted two bikers breaking off and coming around the right side of the compound. I left Frank and Sandra at the front gate, and McCormick and I took one of the walkways to the right side of the compound.

We were making our way to the right side of the compound, surrounded by alligators on both sides. We approached the end of the walkway, which ended at the outer metal wall. Before we reached the end, a figure fell from the wall to the right of the walkway, into the alligator den. McCormick and I both froze in shock as we watched the unfortunate man splash around for a few seconds before being attacked by multiple alligators.

The screaming and blood distracted us from noticing Rico landing on the walkway with his AK-47 pointed at us. He shot the younger McCormick, and he dropped screaming. Rico pointed his rifle at me and told me to drop mine, which I did.

"Hands up. Where is my brother, you bastard?" Rico asked nicely.

"I have no idea who you're talking about, Rico."

"You better figure it out quick, or I end your screaming friend," was Rico's reply.

"You must be talking about the two lookouts you had spying on us. They really shouldn't smoke while spying. They are tied up but safe for now."

"Why are you dressed like that?" asked Rico.

I had forgotten about my cowboy outfit. I wonder why Frank and McCormick didn't mention it.

"You have made a huge mistake. You've killed and wounded a lot of my men, you kidnapped my brother, and you have insulted me repeatedly. I don't know how many people you have lost. All you had to do was leave. Everything you and your group have accomplished I am going to destroy. Why? For what? You should have just left. I showed you respect since you showed me respect in prison. You repaid my kindness with deceit and bullets. All your hard work is going to vanish. I am going to end you and all of your group, including your children. This is the end of your group's story. This is the end of your bloodline. Your actions are going to cost you everything."

While Rico was giving his soliloquy, I absentmindedly reached for my breast pocket to get my lip balm. All the talking and thinking made my lips dry; the fake mustache didn't help either.

Rico moved his rifle up as I reached for my lip balm and told me to freeze, which I did. "Drop it you idiot," Rico demanded. I sure get called that a lot lately. I dropped my lip balm, and it slowly rolled toward Rico.

"You are going to take me to my brother now," Rico demanded and there was an increase in gunfire from the front of the camp.

"Weiner, report in. Did you neutralize the threats?" Bruce screamed through the radio.

Rico started to advance towards me, asking, "Why do they call you Weiner?" Rico looked pretty rough with all the walking he had been doing today. He still had a bandaged arm from the earlier bullet wound, and he still stank of vomit. Rico was not being very careful when he stepped on my discarded lip balm, and his foot went out from under him. He fell hard on his back, and his head hit the metal walkway hard.

"Holy crap!" I eloquently assessed the situation.

McCormick snorted, apparently he was not hurt badly enough that he couldn't react to what happened. Rico was out cold, if not dead. I went toward the younger McCormick, but he waved me off, saying, "Check on the twit first, make sure he isn't getting up." I went to Rico and grabbed his rifle and took his pistol from his belt. He was still breathing, but there was blood coming from one ear. I tied his boot laces together, took his belt off, and zip-tied his wrists together. I then went and checked on McCormick.

McCormick was hit on the side of his chest but may have been lucky enough to miss his major organs, or he was just really tough. I bet he had a tough guy first name. "What's your first name?" I asked.

"Most people call me Ray," he replied.

"As in Raymond?" I asked hopefully.

"No, Ray is short for Razor," he responded.

Damn them all. I helped him up and started our walk back to the central compound. As we approached, we thought we heard sirens, which was confusing. We heard a noise from behind us and turned in time to see Rico clumsily regain his feet and attempt to take a step. His pants dropped to his knees, and his tied shoelaces prevented him from doing more than falling flat on his face with another loud bang. His nose was very likely broken, and from the sound of the fall, he was probably missing teeth. He ceased to move, and we continued to the center compound and the sounds of sirens were getting louder.

Chapter 47: News From Near And Far

I sat Ray down in the compound and checked his wound again. It did indeed appear to be a lucky hit, and I hoped he would be okay with medical attention. I radioed to Bruce to see what was going on.

Bruce informed me that while I was away from the gate, the bikers increased their push to the wall, which resulted in their taking multiple hits. They then retreated back to where they left their wounded. Soon after they reached their wounded, a couple of old-fashioned police cars turned down the driveway with sirens blaring, followed by three old pickup trucks. The police cars looked like they were from a museum. The convoy stopped at the bikers, and a swarm of people in uniforms surrounded the bikers, who surrendered without a fight.

"Oh crap, is our channel secured Riggs?" I asked

"Should be Wiener," responded Bruce.

"Dress the visitors and dump them out back now," I suggested to Bruce.

"On it," was the quick response. "We have time, with all the nails on the driveway. Looks like four of the officers are walking down the driveway to us," Bruce informed me.

I radioed for everyone to put their weapons down and stash the fully automatic rifles. I asked Cathy to come look at Ray, which caused some confusion until I informed them of the younger McCormick's actual first name.

Bruce went to dress and dump the two spies we had tied up. He radioed for Spirit to come help him. They met in the visitor center lobby and entered the small, locked room that held the two spies. Both spies were as we left them, in their underwear tied to chairs. "You cut the zip ties on their feet first while I cover you," directed Bruce. Once their feet were free, they kicked and thrashed. Bruce smacked them both sternly on the head with the butt of his rifle. "Knock it off, or we will tie you both back up and feed you to the alligators."

"I am not really comfortable cutting them loose," Spirit stated.

"I have just the thing. Wait here and cover them," Bruce said, leaving the room.

He returned a few minutes later with a small jar and a cloth. He opened the jar and soaked the cloth in the liquid contained in the jar. Bruce then walked behind one of the bikers and put the rag over his mouth. The biker kicked and screamed for a minute, then went slack. "Chloroform." was Bruce's one-word statement.

"I don't want to know why you have that," said Spirit.

"I use it on larger feeder animals, so the alligators are not harmed when I feed them live animals. Sounds creepy, but it is safer for the gators, and I hope it reduces the suffering of the feeder animals," Bruce explained. He cut the zip ties from the bikers' wrists and stated, "Give them a minute and they will start to come to, but they will be really groggy and easier to control."

Spirit grabbed the bikers' clothing while Bruce got them standing up. "We wasted too much time, we'll dump them at the back gate, and they can dress there." They pushed them to the back gate, shoved them onto the path, dropped their belongings on the ground and closed the gate. Bruce left Spirit to guard the back gate while he rushed back to the watchtower to see what was going on.

While Bruce and Spirit were getting rid of the spies, Cathy and I were helping Ray. Cathy stopped the bleeding and agreed that he got lucky with the wound, but he needed to go to the hospital soon. I figured I better go check on Rico and left Cathy with Ray.

Rico was exactly how I left him, face down, pants down, tied up, stinking of vomit, and missing a few teeth. I untied his shoelaces and cut off the zip ties. As I was trying to pull his pants up, I heard, "What in the hell is going on here?"

I turned to see two uniformed men with Sandra and Frank, all staring at me. Pretty sure I heard Sandra mutter, "Idiot," under her breath. I dropped the still pantless Rico to the ground and stood up.

"Why are you dressed up like that?" asked one of the officers. Next shootout I am just going to go with casual attire. I snatched the fake mustache from my face, which hurt more than I expected. "Officer Smitty, go check on that man, please. You step away from him." I obeyed the command as Officer Smitty checked on the still-breathing Rico.

"It's Rico. Beat to hell, but it's him," stated Officer Smitty.

"Good, cuff him. I'm Officer Dale of the Florida State Police. Who are you?" asked the state trooper.

"I am Jack Emily. How did you guys know to come?" I asked.

"Your neighbor, retired FBI agent Gilbert Fountain, contacted us via shortwave and informed us of your plight. We have been working with the local towns to form an area wide police response team to maintain as much order as possible. We were aware of Rico and his gang terrorizing the area. A religious group and some local citizens were reaching out for help with them. Lucky you guys put up some resistance. We have a local television station up and running on a limited time schedule. Haven't you been monitoring the TV stations?" Officer Dale asked.

"Gilbert is ex-FBI?" was all I could think to say.

"We hadn't bothered with the television for a while now. We spoke to local preppers about the outside world. We hear the larger cities are in chaos and zombies are roaming the world," stated Sandra.

"Those aren't zombies, there are some bad drugs going around that seem to cause long-term and maybe permanent psychosis with some individuals. Yes, the larger cities are in chaos, but we are trying to establish order. You shouldn't put too much faith in those crazy preppers' reports. Why are you dressed like a cowboy? What the heck happened to Rico, and is that blood in the alligator enclosure?" Officer Dale asked.

Chapter 48: Revelations

Rico was taken out with the rest of the bikers. The two spies had made it back to one of their original campsites and were high as kites when the officers found them and took them into custody. They babbled on about being kidnapped and that they were the victims here. The spies stated they were actually doped up by us before they decided to get doped up with their own stuff.

Ray and Steele were transported to Dixon City for medical help. We were informed part of Dixon City was back under control and minor services were available. Apparently Dixon was under the control of an organized crime group, but the former mayor shot and killed the ringleader, and the rest of the group was soon taken out, and the mayor was restored to power.

Officer Dale and Smitty remained to take our statements. We proceeded to tell them our story, leaving nothing out but Pantless Poncho Zombie Guy. When we finished, they brought us up to speed on the local happenings.

They informed us the prison was still running but bare bones. Many of the staff were living in the prison for now. Officer Dale had been in communication with the jail and was aware of who I was. The officer reported there were a lot of inmate deaths due to the flu. Officer Dale mentioned that he had made a run to the prison just before the solar flare knocked everything out. He was called to help transport a prisoner to the Grantville City Hospital. The inmate's ear had been bitten off by another offender. He reported the ear was missing for a while but was later found on the bottom of one of the SRT team's boots. He further informed us that the prisoner tried to escape through a broken window on the third floor. Earlier that day a drug-induced psychotic patient had thrown a chair through a window. The inmate was apprehended before he could escape.

Officer Dale reported that Grantville fared the best out of all the local towns and was doing well maintaining law and order inside most of the town. It had some problems with groups like the bikers attempting to raid the town from time to time but was maintaining control at present. This could be a bigger problem if the raider groups grew in size. He also informed us that food was becoming harder to get, and people were getting desperate.

Officer Dale warned us that the dangerous drugs were still being spread and it was difficult to warn people even with a television station transmitting part-time. Most citizens did not have any power or functioning TVs or radios. They were also on the lookout for a Grantville business owner who was selling the tainted drugs on the side. He was last seen with a group of hippies at Hippie Fest wearing a yellow and red poncho.

The officers informed us that the kids were safe at the Fountains' house. They reported that retired agent Gilbert "The Fist" Fountain had instructed the State Police in karate for many years. Officer Dale reported that Agent Fountain got my message and reached out to the State Police, and they organized a group to subdue the bikers and help us.

"Gilbert is ex-FBI? His nickname is The Fist?" was all I could think to say.

"The countryside is very dangerous, and part of Dixon is still pretty sketchy. Crystal City is pretty out of control, but citizens are banding together and trying to restore order. Grantville is doing pretty well but has minimal power, and they are bartering instead of using money. Food is becoming an issue everywhere, and the drugs are still coming into the area. So, the amount of drug-induced psychosis is still increasing. The flu is running through most of the towns, and there have been a lot of deaths attributed to the sickness."

The officers reported that they picked up a few of the hippies that were wandering around when they arrested the bikers. We had shot seven of the bikers, one of whom was mortally wounded. They reported that five hippies were killed by the bikers. Three of the hippies and two people from a religious group were killed earlier in the week at a campsite, and two hippies were killed earlier today.

"If you travel, be well armed, go in a group, and be vigilant. We are on the cusp. Things could get better or worse depending on what the majority of people decide. With food getting more and more scarce and the tainted drugs still being used, violence will likely increase. If you need anything, I suggest you go to Grantville and do it soon. Things could get better, but I suspect not soon. Oh, and watch the darn television and talk to the preppers a little less," were Officer Dale's parting words.

Chapter 49: Reunion

The next morning Cathy and I got on our bikes and took the trail back to our house. We checked the houses, fed the animals, and then walked to the Fountain family's house. When we neared the house, I radioed in, hoping they were monitoring the radio I had left on their doorstep.

Gilbert responded immediately and told us to come to the front door. We were invited inside and greeted by the kids, Gilbert, Jane, Timmy, and Graven. We hugged the children and thanked the Fountains repeatedly for taking care of the kids and sending help. We were so overjoyed with seeing the kids, it took me a minute to realize Graven was here and alive.

"Graven, I thought you were dead!" I tactfully stated.

"What fool told you that?" he asked.

He had a good point. Instead of answering the question, I asked him what happened to him and Tiffany Steiner after leaving our house that fateful night.

He told me that he had taken Tiffany to the emergency room and sat with her until she was admitted and waited for her father to arrive. He left the hospital around 3:30 am. He reported he was walking to his car, which was parked in front of the police station. There was a disturbance in the street in front of the station, and he pushed his way past a couple of people wrestling by his truck. Graven reported he had to knock a druggie wearing a blue hoodie to the ground to get to his truck. Graven stated he then jumped in his truck and drove home.

When the power went out a few days later, he walked up to the Fountain's house and agreed to team up and help each other protect the area. Gilbert had informed him that we would likely team up with Bruce at the alligator farm and that end of the "neighborhood" would be covered.

They had seen the hippies running around the woods, but they never crossed the fences, so they avoided contact with them. The hippies seemed to help patrol the area and keep intruders away. They left some food out in the hopes the hippies had enough sense to eat. As time progressed, they saw more people traveling the roads and trails on foot and heavily armed.

Gilbert and Graven assumed many of the travelers mistook the hippies as people patrolling the area.

Graven reported that a few days after the power went out, and before Grantville started to get too chaotic, a couple of police officers in an old pickup truck came looking for me. Graven informed us they were driving up and down the road looking for my house but could not locate your mailbox. Oops. He said they finally flagged them down and spoke with the officers. The officers stated before the power went down, they had seen video footage of me being attacked by man with a knife on their CCTV camera. The officers wanted to let me know that they had the offender in custody and wanted a statement from me. Graven told them he would pass the message on if he saw me, but did not tell them about the alligator farm.

We traded shortwave radio contact information. We walked back to our house with the kids, loaded up the bikes, and went back to the alligator farm.

Chapter 50: Research

We decided it was time to send a small group to Grantville to obtain supplies and gather information. Since Steele was still healing and Bruce was in charge at the compound, I was the obvious choice to lead the expedition. Sondra volunteered to go, but only if she was placed in charge and I did not go. She was always jealous of my natural leadership abilities and my being able to think on my feet. The group agreed to let her lead, but Cathy and I would have to accompany her.

We were running low on some supplies for the ladies of the group, and we wanted to see how the town was running for ourselves. We packed lightly, and all road bikes that had trailers attached so we could bring back whatever we needed. We had two options, look like we had nothing worth taking or look heavily armed and dangerous. We decided that appearing heavily armed and dangerous was the better approach. With two females, we felt it was safer to send the message we were not to be messed with rather than helpless and weak. We opted to wear army fatigues, all carried AR-15s and all had a sidearm on our belts. It would take two days of travel to get to Grantville safely on bikes. We would use trails and back roads as much as possible to reduce the chances of being ambushed or stopped at a roadblock.

Steele begged to go, insisting even with one good arm he was useful. We agreed that he was useful even with one arm and needed to stay and protect the compound. With that settled, we planned to leave before daybreak tomorrow. I had not been to Grantville since the EMP and wanted to visit the Conner Pawn Shop and the O'Brian's Hardware Store to see how my friends were doing.

Early the next morning we left at 4:00 am. We used the roads briefly before switching to the trails. There were many people on the roads and trails, and we hid often until they passed. We saw a large amount of the drug-induced "zombies" stumbling around also. On the first day of travel, we managed to avoid any major encounters. We stopped in the early evening and decided traveling at night would be better with all the travelers out.

We struck out around midnight and were doing well until we met a group that far outweighed our skills. We were traveling through a rather densely forested part of the trail when we found ourselves surrounded by a group of twelve soldiers with night vision goggles on.

They demanded we lay down our arms and step forward. We had no choice but to comply. They gathered our weapons and asked us what we were doing and where we were heading. We informed them that we had spoken to local law enforcement yesterday and were informed that there was some semblance of order in Grantville. We were heading there to seek safety. We knew better than to disclose information about our sanctuary.

The soldiers informed us that they had been isolated on base until they received orders to transport some assets to Atlanta. At this point a man in civilian clothing stepped forward. From the way Cathy and Sandra reacted, I supposed you would say he was a handsome fellow. He had short, sandy blond hair and a slight beard and mustache.

He informed us that he was being transported to the CDC to help address the zombie situation. They had a doctor with them that had a theory that the zombies would not attack humans that were infected with a disease. The doctor's theory was that the zombie virus only sought out healthy hosts to spread. Cathy and Sandra just stared at him dreamily and agreed. They introduced us to a dark-complected doctor who mumbled something about nature being a serial killer or something like that.

I told him that was a stupid idea and that they weren't zombies. I informed the fellow that they were just a bunch of druggies running around high as kites. I asked them how long they had been isolated. The handsome fellow reported that they had been isolated the entire time and got all their information from the government and local preppers. They seemed amused at my response and decided we were of no threat and let us continue on our way. We were rearmed and left to continue.

"He looked like that guy from Fight Club," Cathy stated.

"Ed Norton?" I asked.

"No, the other guy," Sandra said.

"Getting sick to avoid getting attacked sounds like a bad idea. Pretty sure those druggies would attack someone with the flu just as quickly as they would a healthy person. Big dummies," was my summation.

We pulled out the shortwave radio to contact the compound. We intercepted a communication between two groups. They seemed to be adversaries, but we only heard the following before it ended.

"O.K. Hey, you, in the mall, listen! We don't like people who don't share. You just messed up REAL bad!" said the first group. The second group appeared to not want to respond. After a few minutes the first group sent another message to the group in the mall. "We're coming for you," was all we heard before we lost the signal, or they just stopped talking?

"We need to keep moving," Cathy said.

We got up and continued down the trail. We continued for a few hours. Twice during that time, we had to drag our bikes into the woods and hide while groups passed us. Around 5:00 am we arrived on the outskirts of Grantville. We decided to scope the town out. If all looked well, we could attempt to enter the town when the sun rose.

Chapter 51: Entry

We watched the main road leading to the town. At daybreak, groups of people started traveling on the road. There appeared to be a checkpoint at the entry to the town, but the foot traffic was flowing well in both directions. They seemed to be allowing people to enter with their weapons. We got onto the road and biked toward the town. We were stopped at the entrance, and they requested our names and IDs. They asked us what business we had in town and when we planned on leaving. We complied with the requests and told them we would not be here for more than twenty-four hours. They told us to leave by this exit and sign out, or they would come looking for us. They told us not to forget to sign out upon leaving, or we may not be allowed back in.

After getting through the checkpoint, we walked our bikes to the market area set up in the town center and purchased as much of the supplies that women needed as we could afford. There were many people in the market, and some had that "Mad Max Road Warrior" look. There were multiple armed guards to help keep the peace. After we finished with the market, we went to O'Brian's Hardware store.

Upon entering the store, there was no singing, and most of the shelves were empty. Rick Plumber was in the store as usual, though not his chipper self. He seemed to perk up when he saw us and asked how we were doing. I asked him where the group was. He stopped smiling and said one of the four was shot and killed in a robbery early into the power outage when things were really crazy. One died of the flu, and the other remaining quartet member left town to wait things out at his cabin with his family.

Rick reported things were very dangerous the second week of the power outage. He reported the town was still very volatile, and he sleeps here most nights to guard the store. He recommended we get what we need and get out of here. We asked him if he needed anything.

"I'm doing pretty well, but I could use some more 9mm ammo," Rick responded.

"Well, you are in luck," I told my friend and gave him two boxes of 50 rounds. He attempted to pay us, but we refused. Though the ammo was as good as gold, Rick had always been good to me, Cathy, and the kids, so it was a pleasure.

"Well, let me at least give you something in return. Something I always carried specifically because of you." He went to the back storage area and returned with a case of Yoo-hoos. I teared up a bit.

He always kept a bunch of Yoo-hoos in the back for his vending machine. He told me there were only two customers that drank it, me and some old hermit who lived in the woods and came in once a month to look around and buy a Yoo-hoo before going back into the hills.

We talked a bit longer and parted ways. It was past noon, and we decided to look for something to eat before going to the pawn shop. We went back to the market center and sought out food.

There were multiple vendors selling everything from roast chicken to roast rat. We chose the chicken. We bought a gallon of water, and even though they promised it was purified, we put sixteen drops of bleach into it and let it sit. We wanted to use up the bleach and not use the purification tablets that we also carried. The shelf life of bleach is limited. Sixteen drops are recommended for cloudy water, which this wasn't, but why take chances? After we ate, we headed in the direction of the Conner Pawn Shop.

We approached the Conner Pawn Shop and observed a small line at the front door. When we got there, we saw there was a sign stating that only five customers were allowed to be in the store at the same time. Picture ID was needed to gain entry, only silver, gold, and ammo were used for purchases, with a purchase limit of two boxes of ammo, and no pets.

When it was our turn at the front door, the man blocking the way in looked very familiar. He asked, "How is the wife and triplets?" Oh heck, he was the guy I saw on the side of the road in the middle of nowhere I saw before the power went out.

"This is my wife and her friend Sandra. Thanks for asking, everyone is fine," I answered as I shoved my "wife" and Sandra in the door.

"Since when did we get married, and what triplets?" Cathy whispered to me as I ushered her by.

Sandra just looked me in the eyes and shook her head.

"Good to see you, Jack," Moe said as we entered. "I see you met my younger brother, Al."

Al waved and moved off to help another set of customers.

"He came here from Italy just in time. Thank goodness he was not in a plane when the EMP hit. He has had a rough time with all the traveling. He had to land in New Orleans and rent a car and drive here. All the sitting gave him problems, and he had to pull over every couple of hours to take a break."

That explained the look of discomfort on his face when I met him. I guess you should not jump to conclusions about people. I bet he had to leave Italy because of some mafia thing.

I bought two boxes of 9mm ammo to replace the two I gave to Rick. I also bought a hammer from the tools section. It was on sale. Moe said his store was very secure, and his apartment was upstairs, so he and Al could take care of the place. He said there had been only one attempt to break into his store, but that was "taken care of."

It was close to 6:00 pm, and Moe suggested we either get a room or get out of town before dark. Moe informed us that he and his brother have a place to go not far from Grantville if or when it falls. He urged us to get far from town before setting up camp and have a guard at all times. We thanked him and Al. Al insisted we take three suckers for the triplets as we left. Cathy just smiled, and Sandra murmured, "Idiot," under her breath.

We were heading to the edge of town when Sandra informed us, we had picked up a tail. This confused me at first until she clarified that a group of four was following us. She whispered, "It looks like an older man, two college-aged kids, one female, one male, and a teenage girl. Let's hide in an alley and see if we can give them the slip."

We turned a corner and joined the foot traffic of a busy street. We ducked into an alley that had a dumpster overflowing with garbage and hid behind it. As the followers walked by, we heard the younger male say, "We need to work on our cardio."

The older male said, "We lost them, let's go to the market and get some Twinkies."

After we were sure they had left, we made it to the exit. We checked out and started down the road. We wanted to go a good amount of distance down the road before slipping into the woods and getting on the path. We were about a mile down the road when we saw what appeared to be a large group coming our way. We had just cleared a hill, and there was no time to hide before we were seen.

The man leading the group was wearing a short-sleeve, white dress shirt and red tie. He appeared to have a cricket bat in his hand, and the group behind him seemed to be armed with melee weapons and no firearms. Their group all went to one side of the road and kept coming towards us. They did not present as particularly intimidating, so we lined up on the other side of the road and continued in their direction cautiously.

As we passed them, they said hello with thick English accents. We stopped and talked to them for a few minutes. They were "on holiday" from England when the EMP hit. They were trying to make it to the leader's girlfriend, Barbara's, house in Grantville. The leader said his name was Shawn, and though he introduced his group, it is the only name I remembered other than Barbara. Shawn said his girlfriend had a radio, but theirs had died, so he could not contact her and let her know they were almost at the town. I allowed Shawn to use my radio, and he contacted her. All we heard of the conversation was, "We're coming for you, Barbara." We wished them luck and continued down the road.

As we continued on, we were more careful when cresting hills. As we approached the top of another hill, we heard arguing ahead of us. We parked our bikes and left Cathy to guard them. Sandra and I went to opposite sides of the road and slowly made it to the top. We saw two men pointing guns at an older fellow. The older man had his hands up and was on his knees. The older man was pleading to be left alone. Sandra and I were still some distance from the group, and our rifles had the advantage of being more accurate at this distance.

Sandra motioned for me to point my rifle at the guy on the left, and she took the right. In a loud voice she yelled, "Don't move or we will kill you." Both fools moved, turning around to face us. They saw the rifles pointing at them and raised their hands. The older man stood up, picked up a shotgun that was lying beside him, and cracked one of the thieves on the head with the butt of his shotgun. The other one took off running into the woods. The old man laid his shotgun back down and raised his hands, facing us and smiling.

We approached and took the unconscious man's firearm and zip-tied his hands. We asked if the old man was okay. He assured us he was and asked if we were going to rob him too. We assured him we were not going to rob him, and asked would he guard this man without killing him while we retrieved our bikes and companion. He agreed not to kill the man but said he may kick him a bit.

After we brought the bikes and Cathy to the two men, we asked where the old man was going. He reported that he lived by himself in the woods and only came to town occasionally to get his favorite drink and say hello to his friend at the hardware store. He said he had noticed a lot of people and motorcycle riders running around lately and knew something was wrong. We filled him in on what was happening for the last month. He did not seem upset until we told him that it was dangerous to go to town and urged him to return to his home.

"Once a month I go to town and get myself a Yoo-hoo. It is my only luxury. I figure if I can't even have that, then this world is not worth living on. I know that sounds extreme, but I try to be a humble man, and I ask for nothing from anyone. If I can't have my one simple joy, what's the point?"

Sandra and Cathy both just stared at me. I had vomited up the last of my Yoo-hoos on Rico. They were as valuable as gold. "Okay, okay, fine. I have a case of Yoo-hoos you can have. Just don't go to town and be more careful."

The old man was in shock. He said God must have put us here to save him and give him his one simple pleasure. All I know is God took my Yoo-hoos away, and I was good with that. We gave him the robber's gun, checked the crook's pockets, and gave him the extra ammo and what little money he had on him. We informed him where our compound was, which he was familiar with. He agreed to come to us if he needed help or had questions, not town. The old man went off into the woods with, for him, a twelve-month supply of Yoo-hoos.

"You know, you could have just given him half, right?" asked Cathy.

After a pause, I responded, "Yeah, I know." Damn it, I hadn't thought of that.

Thankfully, the rest of our trip back was uneventful, though we had to hide multiple times to avoid the other travelers. We got back to the alligator farm late in the evening of the fourth day.

Chapter 52: Things To Come

The group met for a late dinner when we got back. The kids, who had the sharpest eyes out of all of us, were in the watchtower. We sat back and had a good meal, sadly without Yoo-hoos.

The local preppers were saying that they were seeing increased hostile activity. Crazy Tom insisted that there were zombies, and that the tainted drug story was just a cover-up. He stated he had been talking to some military guys, and they were working on a way to combat the zombies. We attempted to contact Paranoid Billy, but we had not heard from him in over a week.

We discussed all that we had been through without mentioning the Pantless Poncho Zombie Guy. We laughed at the bizarre characters we had met. We took a moment to honor the loss of life we had witnessed and heard about. We gave thanks for the new friends we made.

The group discussed how much better off we were than most, and if things continued as they were, how much danger we could be in.

We had allies in the area, but the motorcycle gang let us know just how vulnerable we were. Had the police not shown up when they did, and had Rico not slipped and bumped his head, we could have been in a lot of trouble.

"No matter what happens, together we will stand strong. We shall overcome. We will persevere. Together we can move mountains," was my inspiring speech.

"Okay, Braveheart," said Cathy.

"Idiot," Sandra stated.

"Weiner," said Spirit.

"Hey, I liked it," said Bruce.

Our little conflict with the bikers was likely insignificant in the grand scheme of things. Helping those we encountered probably only benefited a few. Good overcoming evil may not impact the world when it happens in a small, isolated town. However, thousands upon thousands of these little positive occurrences all over the world may just have an impact after all.

The End for Now

Afterword

I have read a lot of "End of World" and TSHTF scenario books over the years and loved them. I especially enjoyed zombie and EMP books. Many times I thought, "Heck, I can write a better book than that." This was my feeble attempt at writing a book that I hope many will like, and few or none would despise. This book was intended to be fun, while passing on some useful information along the way. Most apocalyptic books are tense and dramatic (rightly so considering the subject matter). I hope this had enough drama, while still being very human. Many of the books I read had a Navy Seal or Special Forces member as the main character. I picked an average Joe and named him Jack. The field is currently saturated with zombie books, so mine isn't.

A few friends suggested I use Artificial Intelligence to write or edit the book. I have always been anti AI, but I admit, I had a hard time getting started so I typed in my ideas, and out popped a bunch of garbage, but it got me started. There are two or three sentences early on in the book that I altered drastically that were born in the AI sewer. I saw the drivel it pushed out and thought, "Heck, I can write a better chapter than that", but it is what got me moving. My wife picked out the offending sections right away, even after I had altered them. Forgive me for using AI to get started, I promise never to do it again.

Artificial Intelligence is not something I want to be associated with, so I stay away from it. I did not use AI to alter or make recommendations after I wrote the book. I did not hire an editor, because I could not justify using money that should be spent on my wife and children on a book that may only be loved by me and a few close friends. I did use multiple online grammar checkers and had a few educated friends scan it in search of errors.

I enjoyed writing the book, and now worry about the reception the readers will give it. For you serious readers, I hope you found enough information and action to have satisfied your thirst. For those looking for an escape, I hope you found it and learned a little more about how to escape if needed!

Please leave a good review if you liked the book, and no review if you did not like the book. If you liked the book, tell your friends, if you did not like the book, lie to your friends. Do not hesitate to contact me about the movie rights.

Finally, I am no survival expert, and all the sage words of advice given in this book should be taken with a grain of salt. I take no responsibility for the use or misuse of the information bestowed in this book.

Credits

Lethal Weapon 1987 American action film directed by Richard Donner and written by Shane Black.

Monty Python and the Holy Grail 1975 British comedy film based on the Arthurian legend, written and performed by the Monty Python comedy group directed by Terry Gilliam Terry and Jones.

Dawn of the Dead 1978 zombie horror film written, directed, and edited by George A. Romero.

Night of the Living Dead 968 American independent horror film directed, photographed, and edited by George A. Romero, written by Romero and John Russo.

Left 4 Dead 2008 first-person shooter game developed by Valve South and published by Valve.

Shaun of the Dead 2004 zombie comedy film directed by Edgar Wright and written by Wright and Simon Pegg.

Zombieland 2009 American post-apocalyptic zombie comedy film directed by Ruben

Fleischer and written by Rhett Reese and Paul Wernick.

Principles of Personal Protection by Jeff Cooper, United States Marine, the creator of the "modern technique" of handgun shooting.

Evil Dead 1981 American independent supernatural horror film written and directed by Sam Raimi.

John Denver American singer and songwriter.

World War Z 2006 zombie apocalyptic horror novel written by American author Max Brooks.

Fight Club 999 American film directed by David Fincher.

Amazon reviews.

If I missed someone, my apologies.

www.ingramcontent.com/pod-product-compliance
Lightning Source LLC
Chambersburg PA
CBHW070637260626
47161CB00007B/2734